The Outer World

For my mom

Prologue

Back when tigers used to smoke. During the year 2156, we left from a planet called Earth after an infectious parasite landed from on the ship V2-365. Very few humans make it to safety in a bunker. From there this brown monster infected millions of people. Murdering them all within a few weeks.

We were able to send a few million people to the planets of Viridian, Nassor, Pewter, and Valor. After we knew they made it out safely, we blew up Earth destroying the Cuchillo. 200 years later people from planet Nassor and planet Pewter started to expand throughout the galaxy.

The leader Malus of planet Nassor knew the people of Pewter were doing the same thing. So they invaded Pewter and took it down from the inside. To make sure the people from Viridian and Valor wouldn't do the same. They took over the planets and expanded. Creating the U.G.C or The United Galactic Confederacy.

In 2399 the planet Viridian became an industrial slave planet because of their rebellion against the U.G.C and in 2428 the planet Valor was set free to be alone to see how it develops with only minimal help.

On planet Rozz there was an explosion in the year 2693 in its gold mine. Killing nearby families. 26 years old Von lost his Wife and unborn baby in the explosion. His best friend since childhood Seth lost his mother and girlfriend.

President Seaburg unexpectedly called them and told them he had a job for them on planet Valor. Something that would change their lives forever, and the rest of the galaxy. They just didn't know it yet, but how could they have known?

Part: 1

The arrival

Soldiers log number 1, stardate 2694 5 days in. I and Seth just landed on the planet Valor, by the request of Ora Dem-wise. We heard a loud crash as we landed. Steam came from tubes on both sides of the door as it was lifted up. We were then greeted by Ora.

"Hey guys how are you"

Ora has long black hair about 5'8 and slightly bulky. She was wearing a purple button-up shirt, black jeans, and a leather jacket. Out of the corner of my eye, I see a girl about 5'6 with long curly chestnut hair. She was wearing a white shirt with a black jacket and pants. S-

"I'm good how 'bout you". Said Seth trying to break the uncomfortable silence.

"Great! Bly and Zach will take the two of you on a tour" Responded Ora out of nowhere.

Bly's 5'7 with short brown hair wearing a white t-shirt with black pants and a light blue jacket. With a slightly muscular build. Zach's about 6'1 with shorter blond hair. He was wearing the grey military garbs that had a few badges of honor on it. With a hilt of a plasma sword and a standard plasma derringer. From all of that, I barely noticed the very muscular build he has. There are a dozen dull buildings, all 10,000 square feet with many plants here and there. All with the same tan color. But when we got to the end there was a final 13th building with designs that were clearly made with care.

"This is the government building where our Iskels reside," said Bly.

"After this is just woods and fresh lakes". Said Zach.

I looked over in the distance and saw a tower with a logo on it.

"What about that," I say.
"It's one of the N.G.C's watchtowers," Says Zach.
"The N.G.C stands for New Galactic Confederacy, they think the U.G.C is corrupt so they want to take them down" Elaborated Bly.

I got thinking about that point but realised it was not a big deal. I've worshiped the U.G.C my whole life, I don't know how that crossed my mind. I know I need to stop the N.G.C's but I don't think I can. I'm not really a soldier, I was just drafted to be one.
"Oh if I get my hands on one of those guys I'll snap their neck," barked Bly.
"We'll show the two of you your quarters," said Zach.

He brought me and Seth to the one closest to the government building because it's the military one. Every team has its own room. Its size depends on how many there are. Other than that there was a small kitchen with a larger cafeteria next to it and a round training room set on the roof.

The training room had a large screen with areas to exercise, work out, and to train with weapons. But there's a smaller room for mind exercises. Bly said something about an Astral Plane to enter. But only a few people had done it before.

We then went to our room. The other 3 members were there. Dray's about 5'3, very broad and muscular. With short black hair. Raith is 6'0 very lean with slightly long black hair. Last is Syless he's 5'6 a little muscular and has long black hair. They are all wearing black t-shirts and pants.

Syless is very quiet and seems to keep to himself. Raith seems a lot quieter, you can't even hear his footsteps. He's wearing heavy boots too! I don't know how he can

even do that.
"Oh my god! You guys must be Von and Seth, I'm Dray it's so nice to meet you" Said Dray.

That caught me off guard because the others are all very quiet, and he just wouldn't stop talking. I'd like to tell you what else he said but I wasn't paying attention. Though Seth seemed to be pretty into the conversation.
"I'm going to go get some fresh air," I said.

I walked out of the room and through the hall to the outside. Somehow I made my way to a field of flowers. Mainly of the colors pink, purple, and white. I looked up from the flowers and saw a person.
"Hi there, don't I recognize you from somewhere?" asked the woman.

She walked closer to where I could see her and it's the girl from when I first landed a few hours ago.
"Oh you're one of the guys that came down in the ship, I'm Elaine," She said while putting her hand out.
I shook her hand and said, "I'm Von".
"You look like you need a friend, do you want to go out to dinner?" Elaine said.
I then said, "no, I'm a bit busy at the moment."

We just had a conversation, but I got uncomfortable and left. Eventually I was able to make it back to the room with the others. They were all staring with these blank eyes. They were definitely confused.
"You ok?" said Syless
"What's wrong," said Dray in a worried tone.
"Oh nothing, it's just really cold outside," I said while pretending that I was shivering.
"Yeah right," said Zach in a sarcastic tone.

He then left, not saying a word, I'm starting to wonder what's up with that Zach guy. Well at least he talks, unlike Raith or- well I guess Syless did just say something just a minute ago.

But now that I'm a part of the team I should get to know them better. But it's already night, the cycle is a lot faster than it is on my home planet. A few speakers in the room started to crackle alive.

"Hello people, I'm sure you're aware it's late so we're going to turn off the lights and go to bed," said the person on the speakers.

I laid down trying to go to sleep but I just kept thinking about that day. I lay there for hours, but still nothing. But after a while, I drifted off. Starting to hear a woman sing.

When the wind blows
Deep at night
Sitting by a fire
Warmness on my feet
Before the wind dies down
But at least I still
Have you besides me

When the wind blows
Deep at night
The fires gone out
I then grew cold
But at least I still
have you besides of me

When the wind blows
Deep at night
Days almost near
The winds gone down
But you're still beside me

The winds gone out
The sun is rising
Day's finally here
But before I knew it
You were no longer
Besides me

I looked around in this dreamland, everything is black and white. I saw a pregnant woman sitting on a porch knitting. Wait, that's my porch, and that's my wife. *Whoosh!* Several U.G.C attack ships flew overhead.
It then clicked in my head that today was that day.
"Look out!" I screamed.

But she didn't even flinch.
"Martha!" I screamed at my wife again but nothing.

I walked over, she couldn't hear me, she couldn't see me. I ran over to her shaking her. But she didn't feel me, She just kept knitting. I looked up at the mine knowing that any minute it will explode. Another round of the fighter planes came overhead, and I knew it was time.

Kaboom! I went flying backward watching my wife disintegrate in front of me. All that was left was her charred corpse. I can't do this, I can't be a soldier, I can't beat the

N.G.C's. I'm worthless. I don't know why Ora wants me here, I have nothing of worth. I was just a gate guard on my planet. I've never even shot a gun before, and she thinks I can help? I can't do this.

I woke up panting.

"You ok?" said Syless.

"Yeah, I guess," I said.

After that, I couldn't sleep for the rest of the night. I just laid there doing nothing. I got up that morning, somehow I managed to doze off for a little bit. All I can think about is that song. Oh what was it called, I just can't think of what it is called. Dray came over and got me to go to a waterfall. Just through the woods. We left at 6:30 in the morning. Then the two of us walked 6 minutes through the woods until we encountered a river. We hiked up for 2 minutes until we reached a semi-circle of trees around the waterfall. It was the most beautiful thing I've ever seen.

We went and sat down on some rocks. The waterfall crashing down behind us. It was hard to hear his words, but I managed to get an understanding.

"You don't think you can do this huh," said Dray.

"No, I don't think that I can do this," I explained.

"But you can," said Dray, "you can do it."

The more I looked at him, the more I noticed there was something different about him. His skin was much darker than everybody else on this planet..

"You're not from here, are you?" I asked.

He stared at me blankly, I clearly caught him off guard, "yes I'm from planet Azalea," stated Dray.

I think I remember hearing about that planet.

"That's the planet with the beautiful forests, right?" I said.

"Yeah, it is," said Dray.

"I've always wanted to go there," I responded.
"No, you don't," replied Dray, "it's filled with religious zealots."
"Right, wasn't there a famous school there?" I asked, "something about people called the Menoi?"
"Until they were all murdered, well, mostly murdered," stated Dray.
"That sounds terrible," I responded.
Dray replied, "I've never been a big fan of violence."
"Aren't you enlisted in the war against the N.G.C?" I asked.
"As a doctor, I'm here to help people, not kill them," stated Dray, "I've never been a big fan of war."
I responded, "I've never been a big fan of killing."

After that, you could tell he was going to say something else. Something important, though it took a few minutes before he did.

"What's bothering you?" asked Dray.

This caught me off guard because I wasn't expecting it. At first, I didn't want to say anything. But I ended up spilling all my guts out, and I don't know why.

"Why'd you and Seth come here?" said Dray unexpectedly.
"Ora wanted me to come and stop the N.G.C's," I stated, "Why are you here?"
"I was a part of that school in Azalea, I escaped before they could kill me," said Dray seriously.
"That's awful," I stated.
"I guess I should say they kicked Ora and I out before the murders even came," responded Dray.
"Why?" I asked.
"I got kicked out because I defended Ora," said Dray.
"Why did you defend her?" I asked, "couldn't you have done it in a way to not get in trouble?"

"Well, I don't know," said Dray, confused.

It was a sad story, I wasn't really expecting that. I should have been more specific when I said I wanted to get to know them better. We decided to get back because it was already 7:30.

It was quicker to go back because It's downhill. It was nice and quiet, with no conversations. The only thing you can hear is the birds chirping. In the melody of- of that song, oh what is it called. I kept playing it over and over in my head but nothing. Why is that song so important to me? How do the birds know what it is? Maybe it's just in my head, maybe I'm just going insane.

When the wind blows
Deep at night
Sitting by the fire
Warmness on my feet
Before the wind dies down
But at least I still
Have you besides me

When the wind blows
Deep at night
The fires gone out
I then grew cold
But at least I still
have you besides of me

When the wind blows

Deep at night
The days almost near
The winds gone down
But you're still beside me

The winds gone out
The sun is rising
Day's finally here
But before I knew it
You were no longer
Besides me

I just don't know what that song is called. Before we got in the door.
Dray said, "we don't need to do this".
"What?" I said.
"War we don't need war," said Dray.

Dray's point was interesting, I wouldn't be here if it wasn't for the U.G.C's skirmishes with the Zepher's.
"It's just so dumb," said Dray dumbfounded.

He walked away fastly into the building, clearly upset. I followed soon after but he was already out of the hallway into the room. I'm still trying just to figure out that song. I sat down in the hall and started singing it.

When the wind blows
Deep at night
Sitting by the fire
Warmness on my feet
Before the wind dies down

But at least I still
Have you besides me

Have you besides me
You besides me
Besides me

Wait! That's it! The song is called Besides Me, it was right there, and I didn't see it. Though I think there was another part to it. Oh, but what is it? I have no idea. I walked into the room and Syless was playing guitar. It's a crimson Vindier guitar with horns and a dark-colored wooden neck, with a black pickguard and Leather strap.
Syless then said, "man you got Dray going," while continuing to pluck the strings.

I looked around and Syless was the only one in the room. Somehow Dray wasn't here either. Maybe he didn't come here.
"Where are the others?" I asked.
"I don't know, why would I care?" stated Syless.
"Care for what?" asked Seth as he walked into the room.
Syless responded, "wherever the hell you guys are".
"That's a nice way to put it," I happily interjected.

Though they didn't seem to care. They weren't even paying attention to me. Probably because they don't like each other.
"Bye Von, bye flamey boy," said Seth.
"They call me the man of flames!" shouted Syless.

Strange that they call him that he probably did something to deserve the title.
"Why do they call you that?" I asked.

“I lit a bunch of the Zepher’s on fire, even destroying one of their posts,” explained Syless.

The Zepher’s are the enemy of the U.G.C, and the reason the N.G.C’s are here. The big bad guys, I heard they use currency. You have to pay when you go to the doctor. Such a flawed system, not fair at all, what if they can’t pay? “Leave, I'm trying to concentrate,” said Syless out of nowhere.

So I left the room,“Hello, you need to pick out your weapon,” said someone from behind me.

I turned around and it was Raith, so I followed him down the hall and up the elevator to the training center. He then escorted me to the gun rack. There are four different types of guns.

The first one I decided not to use is the plasma sniper. A one-foot beam of plasma shoots up to 90 kilometers. It’s really good but big and bulky.

Next to go is the plasma shotgun, where a beam gets shot into a bunch of mirrors and shoots out eight different eight inch beams. Though it can backfire easily and blow up. Not to mention it’s hard to pump it so the mirrors are in the start position.

I thought the plasma rifle was good. But it uses a burst system. Instead of it continuing to go. It’s only that way because- it's only like that to stop it from overheating. If it did overheat it would cause the gun to blow up. I sighed at the limited technology.

Which leaves the plasma derringer. It has one beam that goes out in a straight line for eight seconds. If you were close enough you could blow up a ship from space on the ground, if you modified it. If you modify it could extend how long the beam lasts. It could be devastating, but after a while it would just blow up as well.

It definitely seemed to be the best choice for me. When I picked it up he gave me a look. Almost as if he was going to say seriously.

"What? It's light and versatile" I said.

He gave me a slight smirk.

So he said, "ok then".

As we were walking back that song started to slip back into my head. Though something was off about.

The air is steady
In the mid-day
A drop of rain comes down
Sending chills down my spine
The sad thing is that
You're not besides me

That was it, well at least part of it.

"Hey man, want to check out the ruins behind the government building?" Asked Seth as I walked inside the room.

We walked out and then around the government building. It is the remains of an old temple. With burn marks across the 3 remaining columns. You could tell someone blew it up, but why? There was a headstone, so I got closer to read it.

The remains of this temple are,
hereby protected under the U.G.C's conservation law,
For the memories of Borris, Tryte, Tren, and Lenny,
Who sacrificed themselves

To stop Malus,
A so-called "god" of this world,
By blowing up this temple,
Killing both them and Malus,
Because of them, we are on this planet today.

I think it's pretty interesting, I'll read up on it sometime.

"There's something that's hidden here," said Seth almost as if he could sense it.

"What's this?" he said while looking at a metal triangle sticking out of the ground.

He bent over to pick it up. It must have been heavy because he was having trouble lifting it. It was a giant shield four-feet tall and two-feet wide. With a few golden swirls across the edge, and is cut eight inches almost down the middle. With a golden arrow and crest on it the rest filled with silver. Images sparked in my mind when I touched it, a knight-like figure with horns curling down. And a bunch of holes in his armor, part of his body was split almost down the middle. Just like the shield.

Seth then punched the air with it on his arm. *Zoom!* The shield made. Almost as if it was some kind of magic. The shield was so heavy that when he moved it back, it hit a pillar making it crumble. Seth started putting the shield back in the ground as Syless walked by.

"What are you doing?" asked Syless.

"S-sorry we found it underground, and it was kinda heavy so it swung back and broke it," I responded shaking.

He then looked at Seth who was still burying it. "Did he do it?" asked Syless while pointing at Seth.

I then shook my head yes, so he had to cuff us both. I finally saw the inside of the government building. Not for a good reason though. We sat in a stone cell with two wooden benches. Sitting there for at least two hours.

I was released because I didn’t do anything. But Seth had to wait to be prosecuted. Eventually, he was let go because the hearing decided it was an accident. He was lucky for that. After that I decided to go to the library. I had to walk to one of the citizen buildings because the military building doesn't have one. Which I find extremely dumb.

I walked down a few aisles until I found the history section. I searched through until I found the book, The Hero, the God, and The temple. I also picked up The Hawks Arrow and The Giants Shield. I checked them out and also bought a leather satchel to put them in.

I made it back to the room in 5 minutes and put the satchel on my bottom bunk. I don’t know why we have four bunk beds, we have enough room to put eight regular beds in. Though it would be pretty crowded. So I guess it makes sense for it not to be that way.

I guess I had been sitting there for a while because Raith and Syless were staring at me blankly. I guess that detal doesn't matter. I decided to go back up to the training center to practice. I don’t know why I didn’t do it when I was there, I guess I was just to busy being arrested

I picked up a plasma sword from the wall. And I began to swing it around a little bit, before slashing a mannequin across the chest. The whole thing went up in flames before falling to the ground. I then stabbed another one through the eye, melting that side of its head off.
“Man this thing’s pretty good,” I said.

I then swung it around in a figure-8 motion. Cutting

the legs off another one, and when it was on the ground I stabbed it through the chest. It went up in flames, creating burn marks on my sleeve. I threw it up and caught it with my left hand. Afterward, I cut one of the heads off and it went up in flames as well.

My jacket sleeve also went up in flames, and I dropped the plasma sword but thankfully it shut before it hit my foot. If the plasma edge wasn't off it would have gone through my foot. I tried patting the fire but my other sleeve just caught fire.

I went to take the jacket off as my back caught on fire. Colors swirled through my head as I started to feel dizzy. I crashed into what felt like the ground and my ears began to ring. I started flailing around until I slipped and fell on the ground, I could feel the flames on my arm quickly disappear before I blacked out.

I woke up in a hospital bed, with a doctor at the edge of the bed. He told me that I had a minor burn on my left forearm. But most of the damage was in my right foot where the sword landed. It was a very deep gash. So I had to wear a cast that goes just below the knee. He told me I also had to use a cane.

Ora walked in and said, "Hey man how are you?" Before sitting down on the edge of the bed.

"I thought I'd be worse off," I said.

"Well when you caught on fire and dropped the sword, you fainted when the blood started coming out," said Ora

"Yeah, I don't really like blood," I responded.

It's kinda funny because I'm supposed to be a soldier now, oh well.

"Well that's not good, I need you to be a soldier," said Ora.

"I know I know," I responded.

Ora then said, "So the next time a mission is called we are going to stay behind, and I'll teach you something."

It seemed fair considering the circumstances. Though I wonder what she's going to teach me. Probably something interesting, maybe something many people don't know. But a lot of people don't know much anyway.

"Ok your time is up," said a doctor.

Ora got up from her seat and left, Syless coming in soon after, I don't see why they all can't come in at the same time.

"I think you deserve my title now," he said jokingly.

I guess I was the Man of flames.

"I'm sure you'll get the title back," I said.

So Syless responded, "I hope not".

We both got a chuckle out of that one. He then left after that, I don't know why. I couldn't get any more visitors that night because of how late it was. I'm surprised I was able to go to sleep because of all the pain I was in.

I ended up back in that dream world. The only different thing was the sky. It was a light blue now, I even heard that lady-Martha was singing.

When the wind blows

Deep at night

Sitting by the fire

Warmness on my feet

Before the wind dies down

But at least I still

Have you besides me

When the wind blows

Deep at night
The fires gone out
I then grew cold
But at least I still
have you besides of me

When the wind blows
Deep at night
The days almost near
The winds gone down
But you're still beside me

The winds gone out
The sun is rising
Day's finally here
But before I knew it
You were no longer
Besides me

The air is steady
In the mid-day
A drop of rain comes down
Sending chills down my spine
The sad thing is that
You're not besides me

She-Martha was a lot better of a singer this time. The gap between her singing and the explosion makes a lot of sense now. Before it was just weird, but not worthy of mention. It makes a lot of sense now, a lot less in between this time than the last. Though there are only three stanzas left. I just stood there instead of going up and trying to get her away. So this time I noticed a few more details. Like Martha's sunflower crown with orange tulips in between each sunflower. Also her pearly white dress with flowers on it. She looked like an angel.

"Watch out!" I heard someone yell in the distance.

It was a gold miner, Martha looked up then Boom! I guess I didn't notice last time because I was so wrapped up in it. One of the burnt flowers came over so I looked at Martha and saw her charred corpse.

I woke up throwing up, so I decided to call the doctor.

Ring ring, ring ring

For some reason, it made a bell sound. But the doctor still came over as fast as he could.

"What's wrong? What's wrong!" screamed the doctor.

Tons of doctors were coming into the room. I could barely understand what they were saying.

"Oh-no"

"We're going to have to do surgery," I heard doctors saying.

My ears were ringing and a light shined bright in my eyes. I felt an intense pain in my left arm. Right where the burn is, I felt as if something was put inside of it.

I woke up in the afternoon with all my teammates sitting at the edge of my bed. Now they were all allowed at the same time. Quite a few tubes were coming out of it. With an incision down the whole burn. They probably opened it up to fix something. There was also green along the edges and in the veins. Somehow I got an infection.

"Is it the doctor's fault?" I asked.

So Raith responded, "no, somehow you got the Cuchillo."

The Cuchillo is the brown infectious disease that drove us away from Earth. I don't know how I could have gotten it.

"The shield!" blurted out Seth.

Now that I think about it could be it.

"What shield!" demanded Bly.

"Wait that doesn't make sense," said Seth.

"Someone did it on purpose," interjected Ora.

"Agreed, it all makes sense now," asserted Dray.

No one else knew what they were talking about. I had a general idea but I don't think it's true.

"So do you guys know about music?" I asked.

"No," said Raith and Zach simultaneously before they left.

"Well you're going to have to ask the music man," said Bly.

I asked Syless "do you know the last three stanzas of besides me?"

"No, I only know the first 2 stanzas," said Syless sadly.

Funny how the person into music doesn't know a whole song.

"Do you have any music books?" I asked.

"No, I go by memory and my own creations," said Syless.

I don't really know how that is a good way to do it.

"Well I'm going to get out of here, get some rest," said Syless.

Why would he say that? I just woke up. It's not necessary to say. I've been sleeping since-since. I looked at the clock and I have at least been out for a day. Once I'm out of the hospital I'm going to go around and ask my teammates. I guess I just have to sit here and wait. After ten minutes I ended up falling asleep. I can't believe I actually listened to that kid, though I was pretty beaten up. Doesn't change the fact that I complied.

I woke up five hours later, I was really hungry so I decided to call my doctor for food. He came in after a few minutes, he was probably tending to another patient.

“What do you need?” asked the doctor.

So I responded, “food would be nice.”

It took him a few minutes so I just sat there and waited. Looking at a wall, a white wall. Nothing on it, only a single scratch. Probably from a knife, wouldn’t want to be a roommate with *that* guy. There’s always *that* guy.

“Here you go,” I heard the doctor say.

It is a turkey sandwich, with green gelatin and water. Not the best meal but I guess it was all he could get me. Apparently I am at level four of the sickness chart. The sickness chart is a chart from one to five and tells you the urgency of it. I would be at a five if they didn’t add the metal plate in my arm that pulls over the Cuchillo. The Cuchillo has a lot of metal in it so It is highly magnetic. It also conducts electricity, so a plasma beam would just tear it apart, not like it would just regenerate anyways.

“Thank you,” I said to be respectful.

The turkey sandwich wasn’t good at all, I think they used whole grain bread. The water was just water, but the gelatin was really good. I went and itched my arm and it started to bleed. So I rang the doctor again.

“What’s wrong?” the doctor said, panicked.

I lifted up my arm to show the blood. So he cleaned it off and bandaged it. I finished off the rest of my food as the doctor left. I fell asleep after that. I think he put a pill in my food. Otherwise, I wouldn’t have fallen asleep 10 minutes later. Or I was just tired, nah, I’d rather be paranoid.

I woke up the next morning with my head pounding, I can’t believe my doctor would put that in my food. I noticed that no one was at my bedside today. The visitor hours probably are not open yet. But today I'm going to take a self-guided tour of the hospital. Hopefully, I'll find something interesting. Or get caught and have to stay in bed with a guard by my door. So guess I'm going to have to be sneaky, I'll set out later today.

I waited for a little bit before I left. Trying not to be suspicious, so I didn't call for the doctor, he only checked on me every one to two hours. But after a while, he stopped, so I decided now was my chance. I got up all sore because I haven't walked in days. I looked through the door and no doctors were insight. So I decided to walk out of the door.

I saw Bly walking down the hall so I ran up to him. I said "hi" out of breath.

"Hey you must be feeling better since they let you get out of bed," he responded.

I could tell he was a little suspicious about it, but he didn't seem to care.

"I want to ask you about that song," I asked.

So Bly responded, "what song?"

"Besides me," I told him.

"Never heard of it," said Bly.

He walked away, and I saw a chart he was standing in front of. I walked up to get a closer look and it said.

Jestus Niefear: priority level 3

Conteace Moss: priority level 1

Dean Dockner: priority level 4

Seen Zooney: priority level 1

Zu Zan: priority level 2

Candice Vroshocky: priority level 4

29

Ackbar Kisealy: priority level 3

Damian Beek: diseased

Von Castor: priority level 2

Level two: why am I at level 2. Is it because I haven't called him in at all today? Well, I guess I'm cut loose today. So I guess I won't get in trouble today. I just got to find Raith and Zach now. I will talk to Ora and Dray later, maybe Ora could teach me that thing.

Zach's probably in the cafeteria, he eats a lot of food. The elevator came up so I walked in as the other guy walked out. The cafeteria is in sector 3, so I pressed the button and It started moving sideways in that direction. I got a little dizzy from it, but it was nothing to worry about. It suddenly stopped and I almost fell over. The doors opened revealing the cafeteria.

I walked in and saw Zach sitting at a table by himself eating a potato. Who eats a single potato, and the skin too. So I walked up to Zach and sat right across from him.

"Hi," I said.

"What do you want?" he said, not even looking up from his potato.

I responded, "about the song."

"Ahh the song," he said

I told him, "it's called besides me."

"Ah yes besides me. I heard of that-a one before. Sitting by fire warmness on feet?" he said.

I shook my head in agreement.

"Do you know about the last 3 stanzas?" I asked.

He said "only too numb-uh, the first one"

"Well thanks for your help," I said.

He responded, "it is not a problem at all."
As I was walking away I said "Oh-uh where's Raith."
"Balcony," he spit out.

I pressed the button to the elevator, it took a few minutes this time. I took the elevator up to the balcony, and Raith was there. Up there I found out the hospital was inside the government building. He was standing there watching out over the whole I guess town. Community. It doesn't really have a name.
"Hi there!" I said.
"I don't know the song," said Raith.

It took me off guard because he's not usually this harsh.
I said, " it's called besides me."

He didn't look back at me, he must be a little mad at me for something. I think I heard a few sobs from him.
"What's wrong?" I asked.

He turned around and hugged me.
"It's all a lie. It's all a lie," he said.
"What?" I said out of confusion.
He said "we will talk about it later"

Raith stepped back, took his ground and wiped the tears out of his eyes.
"So what about that song, besides me?" asked Raith.
I responded "yes."

He stood there for a minute. Probably thinking of the song. Though it didn't look like it was going anywhere.
"Sorry man, I just can't think of it," he said.
"It's okay," I said frustrated.
I said "I'm gonna head back to my room, can you call down Dray for me?"

He shook his head in agreement, so I decided to go

back. I opened the door and saw the layout of the government building. A few cells in the front and a hospital in the back. I wonder why it's like that? I guess it doesn't really matter.

I waited for a few minutes and the elevator finally came up. I stepped in it and it went down and to the side. It took a minute before I got to sector d. I walked down the hall and looked back at the patient's chart. Dean Dockner and Candice Vroshocky were both diseased now. Veck Bosh was added to the list with level 2. I was brought down again to level 1.

At least now I'm really under the radar. I walked down the hall and into my room to find the doctor standing there looking at his watch. I could tell I was going to be in trouble.
"Where have you been!" he said sternly.
So I said "I went to the bathroom, I got a little lost."

He seemed a little reluctant, but he ended up believing it. I'm surprised I got away with that one.
"We need to take a blood test. To see if you have any Cuchillo left in your bloodstream," said the doctor.

I laid down in my bed and he gave me some pills because he's going to put the tubes in my arm. I saw colors swirling and a talking peanut in a top hat, just a normal Tuesday for me.
"Fancy meeting you in here I'm Cocoa," said the peanut while tipping his hat.

I felt the tube go into my arm, I could see the blood coming out in between the colors and Cocoa.
Cocoa said "now let me sing you a song, *Hello my main man, hello my little nu-ut, Oh if you can see now, if you can see now.* ***HOW THEY HAVE LIED TO YOU!***"

That scared me a little bit, who's lied? I twitched a Little bit from the tube being pulled out. At least the stitches didn't hurt because of the anesthesia. When he left with the blood to get the results the anesthesia wore off. After that It only took a few minutes before he made it back.

"There's only a little bit left in the bloodstream. But once it's all stuck to the metal plate we can take it out," said the doctor.

The doctor left, so I just have to sit here and wait for Dray to come. Though looking at the clock, it's like nine so I'll have to wait until morning for him to come. But the blood test is really important, so I would much rather put off talking to Dray than the test. Man, I just realised I forgot to say Ora too. I guess I'll ask Dray for him tomorrow.

I managed to go to sleep without going into that dreamland. Thank god because I don't want to be back in there again. I woke up a few minutes before the visitor hours were open. So I had to sit there and wait watching at that same blank wall. Nothing really changed about it, just the same old wall. At least Dray came before I got too bored.

"Hey there," said Dray.

So I responded with, "hi."

"So what's that song you want to talk about?" asked Dray.

"Besides me," I said.

"Ah besides me, I think I've might of heard that one before," said Dray.

I asked "where?"

"One night when you were mumbling in your sleep," said Dray.

Now that I think about it when I was younger I used to mumble in my sleep. It would make sense that I still would now.

“So you wouldn’t know any other part of it?” I asked.
“No,” said Dray.

His watch went off in a beeping sound to alert him of a mission.
“Sorry I have to go,” said Dray.

So I guess I have to sit here and wait for something to happen. I was staring at that wall when I realised Ora should be coming. To bring me to the training center to teach me something. But to my surprise Zach came instead.
“Sorry man Ora is going to be here in a few minutes. I decided to stay back with you guys to learn that thing, Seth also decided not to go but he had something else to do,” said Zach.

Zach’s watch also rang, Ora wanted to talk to him. He left the room for a minute so I wouldn’t hear. Must be talking about something important. He walked back in with Ora next to him.
“Sorry I was a little late. I had to do something,” said Ora.
“It’s okay,” I responded.

Ora proceeded to sit down at the side of the bed.
“So there's a song you wanted to talk to me about?” asked Ora.
“Besides me,” I answered wearly.
Ora responded,” I don’t know.”

That’s it, that's all of them. None of them know what it is. I don’t know what it is. The whole trip thing was pointless.
“Well let's get to the training center. You better wear a coat because it's raining,” said Ora.

Wear a coat, because it’s raining. What she said, it’s bringing something back to me. We got up and she handed me a brown trench coat. We left and walked down the hall to the elevator. It was a little crowded between the three of us.

We walked out and crossed the way to the military building. We took the elevator up to the training center. It was starting to hail now, glad I'm not out there.
"Brrr it's chilly," said Zach.

That also got me thinking, the next stanza was on the tip of my tongue. I just can't think of it, rain, coat, cold. I-I almost got it, I decided to run the song in my head so I could get the next stanza.

When the wind blows
Deep at night
Sitting by the fire
Warmness on my feet
Before the wind dies down
But at least I still
Have you besides me

When the wind blows
Deep at night
The fires gone out
I then grew cold
But at least I still
have you besides of me

When the wind blows
Deep at night
The days almost near
The winds gone down
But you're still beside me

The winds gone out
The sun is rising
Day's finally here
But before I knew it
You were no longer
Besides me

The air is steady
In the mid-day
A drop of rain comes down
Sending chills down my spine
The sad thing is that
You're not besides me

I-I got it!

The air stands still
In the afternoon
I went to get my jacket
'Cause the rains pouring down
This rain just shows how i'm feeling
I'm cold and
The sad thing is that
You're not besides me

Part: 2

Betrayal found by stalking prey

Captain's log number one, stardate 2694 nine days in. A few days ago Von and Seth landed on this planet, coming from the planet Rozz. Von seemed nice enough. He was talking into a tape recorder so I decided to do it myself. Seth on the other hand doesn't seem trustable at all. I decided not to go up and greet them with Ora because I thought they were going to leave after a while.

When the door to the ship lifted the first one I saw was Von. He is 5'7 with short brown hair. I could tell he worked out a bit. He was wearing a brown leather jacket, a white button up shirt and black jeans. With sturdy brown leather boots.

Seth is 5'8 with orange curly hair and a bunch of freckles on his face. Something was off, it didn't seem right. He was wearing black overalls and a black long sleeve shirt, and black winter boots. I'm going to have to find out what's up with this Seth fellow.

One day Von decided that he should go train. His sleeve caught fire and it caused him to drop the safety plasma sword. It went deep into his foot, so he ended up running into the wall. The impact put out the fire, but it caused him to fall over because he saw the blood come out of his foot. Thankfully the doctors got there quickly enough to get him patched up. I said hi to be nice.

Since I was in the government building I decided to go to the Iskels. The three Iskels run the government. Sure they're old, ugly and look like slugs, but they run the planet. The lead one wearing red can't hear, the one in blue can't see and the green one can't talk. Might be a reference to something. But they are all able to work together using their psychic powers.

I walked down the hall into the elevator. It went up and to the left. It was super dark in the room because if they're exposed to sunlight they'll burn. Like the mythical monsters called vampires from Earth's past. Such interesting creatures made by humans in the past. There is a dim light behind stained glass to illuminate the area.

"Hello," said the red Iskel.

"Greetings," said the blue Iskel.

"Hey there," I said.

"What do you need?" asked the blue Iskel.

I didn't really have anything to talk to them about. Just my concerns with Seth. Guess I'll go with that.

So I responded, "about Seth."

"You sense trouble in him too," hissed the blue Iskel.

"Quiet down," screamed the red Iskel.

They seemed a little on edge today. Especially the green one.

"You better watch him, he could be dangerous," said the blue one.

"Why don't you just shut up!" yelled the red one.

"Don't tell him that!" said the blue one to the green one.

"He can't hear him!" screamed the red one grabbing onto the blue one's neck.

You know what they don't seem on edge today at all. A little calmer than usual. I decided to slip out so I didn't hear any bit more of the argument. They tend to do that a lot. I went into the elevator and started walking down the hall. Von came up to me and asked about a song. I told him no but I really wasn't paying attention because he is not supposed to be out of bed.

But I looked at the sheet and he was only priority level two. So I decided to let it go and not tell the doctors. I left and walked to the military building and into our room. Syless was still playing his guitar.

“Do you know where Seth went?” asked Syless.

I couldn’t come up with a response. So I think he took that as a no. But I haven't seen him anyways. So I guess it doesn't really matter, the point still got across. That is the important part about it. Though now I got thinking that it’s strange nobody has seen Seth.

After that the rest of the day was uneventful. The morning also was until I got a call to go to the meeting room. I walked in, Dray and Raith were already there. Syless came two minutes after I did. We sat down in our respective seats. A government worker came in.

“Your Commander Ora and Soldiers Zach, Seth and Von won’t be accompanying you on your mission today,” said the government official.

As the government official left the 50 inch tv flared to life, showing president Seaburg.

“Hello the four of you, I have a special mission for you guys,” said our president.

“Ugh what is it?” barked Syless.

Only Syless has the guts to talk to the president like that. Though they have always had a rivalry. I think it’s because Syless has always been a trouble maker.

“Today you are going to spy on the N.G.C’s,” said president Seaburg.

“Do you not know how dangerous they are?” asked Dray.

“Yes, but we have a lead that they are going to do something that can destroy all life on your planet,” snapped Seaburg.

“What happened to just burning them alive,” hissed Syless.

“Now go gear up and stop them,” yelled Seaburg.

From there we had to walk to the gear up center. The first layer we put on is a micro titanium infused with cyfier ore. It's light, versatile and very flexible. It can only be broken through if it was hit in the same spot a hundred times. Next is a grey pad layer, it protects you from falls but it can break easily. The final layer is a lighter grey which is the main protection. With only a few places it's not covering. To keep flexibility it comes on in parts so if you hit in the right spot you can kill them. The gauntlets are also made of the same material. Which are finally topped off with fingerless gloves. Next we grabbed our guns, I got my plasma rifle. Syless and Dray grabbed their plasma derringers. Raith of course picked up his plasma sniper.

We trekked through the heavy rain, mud getting all over our leather boots with more of the grey plates protecting the feet. Now I wish I brought my poncho like Raith and Syless. I'm sure Dray is probably feeling the same way. We entered the woods so the rain wasn't splashing down on us that hard. After a minute we made it to the river. With nash fish jumping out because of all the rain. We took the stride down instead of up towards the waterfall.

After a few minutes we finally made it to the bridge. Only a few boards to the end were missing. I put my right foot on which went across two boards horizontally. They creaked as I put pressure on them. I put my left foot on it and it only creaked a little more.

"Good it's fine,"I said while turning around.

The boards then gave out from under me. I hit my chin on a board while I splashed into the freezing cold water. I tried swimming up to get air but the current was too strong. It kept pulling me down. I felt the chill all throughout my body.

I couldn't breathe. I ended up hitting my shoulder and getting snagged up against something. It allowed me to stay above the water surface brushing up against the mud . A stick hit me on the side of my head. So I grabbed onto it with a very tight grip. Struggling to lift myself up. The mud made it very difficult, my feet kept slipping. Everything around me started turning black. It was so cold, I've never been stuck in a river before. But with each kick I inched up the side. The mud was getting everywhere, but I had no control of that. After a while I ended up being pulled up.

I couldn't see anything, it was so cold. I ended up getting slapped, somehow it caused me to be able to see again. Thank god Syless was the one who slapped sense into me. Raith was the one who pulled me up. Syless pressed a few buttons on my gauntlet making it steam me.

"I didn't even know it did that," said Raith.

"They added it after Wess died," said Dray.

Wess was from the planet Saffron, he used to be on our team. Until he fell in cold water. We know he didn't drown because he was wearing a respirator. Unfortunately when we pulled him out he was frozen in a block of ice, probably the reason why he died.

"I think I know a way to get across the river," said Syless.

First we stuck leaves in between my outer armor and the padding layer, to keep me warm. Next we started breaking branches off the trees. Once we got enough we grabbed vines. We were then tying the sticks together with the vines. We made four pole vaults, one for each of us.

Dray started running, stuck the makeshift pull volte into the river and jumped across the river with ease. Legs sticking out in front of him. Syless went next, he was clinging onto it and made him stick the landing with ease. I went next, my posture was more like Syless's except my back was more towards the side we came from. But while I was going to cross the stick snapped.

My feet hit the side of the river bank. But before I fell I grabbed onto Dray's pull volte that he was sticking out at me. I made it up without falling back into the water. A few leaves might have fallen off. Considering I barely made it I was worried for Raith. He's nearly thirty more pounds than I am.

"Can you throw me the other two?" asked Raith.

He caught the first one with ease. But almost fell over trying to catch the second one. He stuck one on his side of the bank, stuck one in the stream, and stuck one on the other side. Now it was his turn to try to jump. We probably won't be able to get him out of the river.

He grabbed onto the first one shimmying down until one foot was fully submerged. But not enough to pour into his boot. He stretched over and was able to grab onto it. The first pole did snap pushing him into the second one. Before I knew it he was slowly falling in. The pole snapped in two places, and he was able to get a hold of the third one. He pushed off the second one and his knees crashed into the mud of the river bank. He then started to slide down into the river. He tried pulling on the third pull to get leverage to pull him up. It snapped causing him to turn around. He was kicking himself into the mud to push him up. But it was only causing him to go down faster. Thankfully his plasma sniper was on him via its strap. He stuck the butt of the gun into the mud. He tried pushing himself up, then he extended his hand. I grabbed onto his hand and started pulling up.

My feet started sinking into the ground. I pulled even harder and ended up hitting myself in the chin. It was bleeding so Dray cleaned it and stuck mud on it to stop the bleeding. Syless grabbed onto Raith's left with his left hand. He then stuck his knife into it. I was startled, especially when blood landed on my face and chestplate.

"I'm going to kill you!" screamed Raith.

He bent his knees pushing him up an inch. His right elbow hit into the ground pushing him up even more. His right hand was implanted in the top of the bank. He then pushed himself up as far as he could. Kicking a few times, getting his gun out of the mud and make him fall into the grass. Dray sat Raith up against a tree. He pulled out the knife as fast as he could so there wasn't as much pain. He cleaned it up and put a gauze over the wound. He removed the gauntlet to make it easier to wrap his hand. He used the gauze to help stop the bleeding. He then added a wrap so the gauze wouldn't fall off. Then replaced the gauntlet back on his arm.

I took a look at him and his armor was covered in mud. Smeared on the chest plate, ab guards, knee pads and shin guards. All over his left arm, a little bit of blood too. I couldn't tell because of the poncho but I know there is a lot on his back as well. At least we got across the river. There is a building in front of us. Though we knew it wasn't the N.G.C's building. It was a temple like what's behind the government building. Except it's not all blown up. Just a little bit of damage.

After that we only had to walk a little farther to get to the N.G.C's camp. As we were walking the rain died down. It was only sprinkleing now. We made it to the fort. Raith scaled up the wall quickly. Though he's used to getting up to tall places like that. I, Syless, and Dray went to find a different way.

We walked around the corner and saw a staircase. It went up to the same layer Raith was at. He could have saved a little bit of energy if he just looked around. We peeked in from cracks from where the stone weathered. Dray sat at the top of the staircase pointing out his gun. To make sure nobody can come and just kill us. Raith was farthest from the staircase.

He switched his barrel on his plasma sniper from two feet to eight inches. Only because it was a shorter distance considering it was right there. He stuck it in to take a shot if he had too. I was next, peeking through the next crack with my gun up if I had to take any shots. Syless was behind Dray as a backup incase Dray goes down.

We sat there for a few hours waiting. Twenty or so came in and sat down. Eleven more came with these robes holding candles. A final one came in. He looked familiar. It was hard to tell because of his helmet and the face paint. I just oh, what does he look like? Well who does he look like?

So familiar, yet so different. I don't even think he's from this planet. I took a look at the armor. It was just like our armor but fully painted black. All of them except for the ones wearing the robes had armor like that. Maybe the robed ones were wearing it underneath.

"Ah e ai oo. Ah e ai oo. Ah e ai oo. Nish kas bosh hash. Nish kas bosh hash." chanted the crowd.

I wondered what they're chanting for. Probably some voodoo stuff.

"Good evening, fellow N.G.C's. Today we are going to reach a foot we have never met before," said the familiar looking one, "something no human has achieved. Today we will resurrect not a human, but a god!"

Cheers came from the crowd. His voice sounded somewhat familiar too. Though it was hard to tell because his voice was muffled.

“Oh that's going to end well,” said Syless sarcastically.

“Now let’s go to the temple and resurrect our god Mortem!” said the familiar N.G.C.

He and the ones wearing robes left. After they left we followed them. We made sure to stay quite a bit of way behind them so they didn't see us. It was easy to follow them from a distance because of the candle light. It took a few minutes but we finally made it to the temple. They walked through the front door.

We looked around and saw a hole in the ceiling. So we decided to scale up to the wall to look through the hole. Raith climbed up a few steps holding onto the ledge. He took Dray’s hand and helped him climb up. Dray took a seat on the roof because there were a few holes in it. With a little bit of rubble in the temple.

Syless got up next with Raith’s help and also decided to stay on the roof. I grabbed on tight to Raiths right hand. I positioned my feet on the wall and started climbing up. I grabbed onto his hand with my other hand too. After a few steps I grabbed onto the edge. Grabbing onto it with both hands as I slipped, nearly falling, a few pebbles and a little bit of dust came down on both sides. Raith put his finger against his mouth and we all froze.

“It was probably just an animal,” I heard one of the guys in a robe say with a growl.

Raith signaled to me to come up. I got up and sat on the part of the roof that was attached to the wall. Raith sat up there too. We were watching it and I realised something.

It was Seth.
"Seth," I said to myself.

Seth shot a wall creating a small explosion. A six foot double headed ax fell from inside of it, along with Mortems casket. It was completely gold with many gems. Sapphires, rubys, emeralds, and precious diamonds. The ones holding the candles took the casket and set it on the ground. Seth set the ax up against a pillar. The ones holding the candles put their candles all around the casket.

One of the robed ones handed Seth a book that had a big eye in the center. It was a brown leather with golden clasps holding it together. It had big green text on it, that read.

The book of the dead
Human sacrifice to the gods

Witchcraft
And resurrections

He flipped through the book until he got to a page and put his finger on it.
"Now as soon as I'm done reciting this," said Seth. "Mortem will be alive once more!"

I pointed Dray's plasma derringer through the hole ready to shoot. Today's the day I'm going to stop The N.G.C's from resurrecting a god. I just needed to wait for just the right moment. To gun him down. While he's reciting the text to resurrect Mortem. I'll be the hero of this story. Like it should be.
"Ni rou dog ew tsurt. Ew era ereh yadot ot tcerruser rou dog

metrom," said Seth. "Fi ew toohs rof eht srats dna yarp ot eht lla ythgim sdog, won si emit ot klat ot ruo sdog."
"Ruo drol dna roivas asafum ereh su won," said the group. "Htiw eht tils fo eht tsir tel su tcerruser metrom."

Now I knew it was my time to strike. The beam struck his shoulder causing him to fall into the pillar. The beam went into the wall behind from where he was standing. He clutched his shoulder. His skin there was definitely burned to the bone. I saw lots of blood come out. The ones in robes took out guns. They looked like they were modified. Probably made them explosive.

Made them explosive! All of the beams hit the bottom of the wall. The whole thing exploded from beneath us. I flew up in the air, pain radiating throughout my body. My shoulder crashed into part of a ceiling, before I hit the ground.

My ears were ringing, and it felt like someone kicked me in my side. I looked up and saw Seth. His helmet was off so I could definitely tell it was him. When the ringing suddenly went to a stop, I kicked him in the knee. He fell to the ground clutching it. I got on top of him, pinning him down. I then picked up a rock ready to smash in his face.

One of the guys in a robe knocked me over dropping the rock on Seth's arm. He screamed in agony as I ignited my plasma sword, going straight through the one in the robe's leg. I took it out causing him to fall over because his leg fell off. Lots of blood was squirting out of it. I stood up and stabbed him through the chest. Another one went to stab me and I slashed his throat. Out of nowhere a beam went along the side of the helmet. Singeing my hair. It hit the column next to me causing it to explode. Knocking me over, my helmet flying off. I fell to the ground with my head throbbing.

I jumped on my feet, shoving the plasma blade through his gut. I heard a *zoom* sound, so I ducked out of the way. The guy I stabbed in the gut had his head come off. I looked up and saw Seth used the ax. I went to hit him with my plasma sword but the ax cut it in half. I kicked him over and he fell onto the casket. I picked up my plasma rifle and shot two of them. Syless, Dray, and Raith shot down the others. My plasma blade regenerated so I went to finish off Seth. He was leaning against the wall, with a knife to his wrist.

I stood there with the rest of the leaves on me, burning to ash. Seth started to move the knife slowly across his wrist. I ignited my plasma sword and swung it. It was about to hit his head when he turned on two of his plasma knives in a cross blocking my shot. So I swung the blade down, cutting four fingers off of his left hand and punched him in his right shoulder. He fell down screaming in agony.

He ignited one of his plasma knives and threw it at me. I dodged it. The blade cut through Syless's left gauntlet, cutting him a little. Afterwards landing into Dray's left foot. When Dray fell down Seth pushed me into the wall. Seth got back up to the casket with his left hand over it. He grabbed the knife and slit his wrist.The blood came rushing down onto the casket and nothing happened.

"It has to be somebody's else's huh?" he asked.

He pushed me into a pillar and grabbed onto my left forearm. He wrapped his other arm around my neck and pushed me against the casket. What I didn't notice was the knife in his right hand. He shoved it into my wrist and twisted down. Lots of blood fell onto the casket. Causing it to glow a deep red.

A humming noise was happening. Dray, Raith and

Syless stepped back. The humming then stopped. Seth stepped back with me still entangled in him. I kicked the casket causing me to push Seth into the wall. So in response he pushed me into the casket. My head throbbed as my stomach groaned in agony. The red on the casket started glowing very bright. The gems on the casket started coming out. They had these things attached to them. Almost as if the gems were screws. That's why it was taking so long.

The coffin door smacked into us and we went flying through the temple wall. Crashing into the grass on the other side. A giant seven foot figure stepped out of the casket. I and Seth laid as still as we could. Mortem had a knight helmet. With devil horns that curled down. Deep crimson eyes. Fashioned in knight armor. Spikes across the forearms and shoulder pads. A three foot long tattered black cape and golden swirl patterns across the armor. He picked up the ax. It had a black handle and a dual sided head. Lined with golden swirls.

“Ishall ki cubye!” screamed Mortem.

He swung his ax with it going straight through the piller. A little bit of the wall and ceiling crashed into him. He didn’t even flinch. Syless, Raith and Dray ran into the woods. Mortem threw his ax at them, not even getting close, at least he was able to knock down a few trees. With a zoom it flew back into his hand. Mortem then started to run after them. I grabbed onto Seth and ran into the part of the woods close to us. They are probably way up north now. So it was best to go to the west. I stuck Seth up against the tree. The hit from the casket must have knocked him out. I stuck a needle into where I sliced his fingers off.

“Ahh,” he screamed in agony as he was swating at me.

So I said, “shh shh, it’s okay, be quiet.”

I wrapped up his hand, with a few gauses on it to stop the bleeding. I got a good look at his armor too. The black paint on it was all scratched off and the left knee guard was off. The left gauntlet was crushed, and there was a hole in his chest plate, a whole bunch of plasma knives attached. I went and wrapped up his shoulder too. The padding was all torn and the armor under was all scratched up. I also noticed my armor. There were burns all across it. A part of the back plate came off. My left thigh plate was off. With a hole in it the underneath armor scratched up. The elbow guard was also off on the left arm. My initial armor was super scratched and cracked. Though my gun and plasma sword were fine.

The suns started to come up. The sky a light purple. With a nice deep orange at the bottom. I pushed a few buttons on my gauntlet. But it didn't work. Must have broken from all the falling I was doing. I sat up all night, not able to sleep because of my pounding headache. By the morning we were both starving. So I grabbed the knife Seth slit my wrist with. I found a bunny straight away.

“Oh, I’m going to get you,” I said softly to the bunny.

I ran over and tried to jump on it. I face planted into the mud. I pulled the knife out of the ground and saw the bunny dart away. I started climbing up a tree branch by branch and I found a sleeping squirrel. I stabbed it through the head, putting the squirrel corpse into my belt to hold onto it. I took out the knife, and heard a crash from under me. Buzzing noise followed from there.

“Oh-no,” I said.

I grabbed onto a vine. Knowing my only choice was to swing tree to tree. I grabbed onto it with my other hand and leaped off the tree. The vine snapped from the pressure of my weight and I landed on my left leg at an angle. The pain was so intense it went up to my hip. I clutched onto it and started to crawl. I felt a sting on the palm of my hand, I ended up squishing the bee into the mud. Allowing me to leap up. I started to jog as fast as I could.

The bees were swarming me so I turned on my plasma sword. I was swinging it around me to kill as many of the bees I could. I managed to get stung in my left cheek and the right side of my neck before I tripped over a tree root. My plasma sword slid out of my hand as I fell to the ground. It cut a tree causing it to fall onto me. My back ached from the tree. The tree might have killed the rest of the bees. I tried crawling out but I couldn't move. I couldn't call for help either, because Mortem would find me. He would be sure to kill me then. I just need to hope Seth comes looking after me.

It must have been hours. Oh I was frantic and so very very nervous. Colors swirled in my head, while someone in there was talking to me. You might fancy me mad. But you have to understand I'm not. How can you possibly say that? My back aching, I was swinging my arms around frantically. The colors were brighter and faster.

I-I felt a tingle in my throat. I needed water. Oh but I can't move from under the tree. I could barely see either. I knew death was stalking me as the day was ending near. I kept getting colder and colder with every waking minute. Death walked closer and closer. I could sense it, the ground shook with every step.

"I'll see you in-," I stumbled with my fist in the air.

As I was about to finish I felt something strike my neck. Oh I know it's death driving his very sickle into me. I felt another one from a different location as well. He carved an x into my neck. Right where he was going to drive his sickle into me. I felt tingles throughout my body. I knew my soul was ascending out of me at this very moment.

I felt another one strike in the very spot. A bright white light seized my eyes. I felt a final strike of a sickle hit the top of my head. I proceed to feel free. My back, no longer aching with pain. The whole world shifted on me, and the bright white light turned into a deep red. This was the devil welcoming me to hell.

“Bly,” said Death himself in a weary tone.

Hell was awaiting my own very arrival. I grabbed onto deaths arm. I didn’t have the audacity to leave just yet. I felt something rub against my eyes. The red disappeared in an instance. The ghostly white light died down. In my blurry vision I could make out what seemed like trees. They had done it. Someone must've found me and saved me from the malady of Death. My eyes shifted back to focus, causing my head to have immense pain. I grabbed onto the top of my head and felt blood. The figure stepped into my field of vision. It was Seth, somehow he managed to sit me up. There were no doctors around, somehow he managed to get me out from under the tree. It was hailing outside as well.

My mind was clouded in dark thoughts. But within the light Seth saved me. Maybe he finally supports the U.G.C’s cause. No longer a traitor. He was a little misguided, but I think he’s starting to turn around. With all the quiet thy mind was seeded, for no longer was I in the presence of satan. But death lurked by, ready for any moment he shall strike. Though I was thankfully a step ahead from death. But then I had an epiphany, why they were heading to the cliff and I know why.

“Let’s stride north,” I said while pointing towards the north.
“That’s south,” said Seth.
“Then that way,” I responded, pointing in the right direction.

My feet stumbled in the tall grass. Seth grabbed my shoulder and started walking me. We ended up at a little pond. He put some of it in a bottle and gave it to me. I gulped down the entire thing in an instance.

Thankfully there were tons of rasp’n-weeds around. Rasp’n-weeds are a mix between a raspberry and a weed. They were bred on this planet and spread like wildfire. I ate several and I felt a lot better. I remembered the squirrel on my belt. So I skinned the squirrel and placed it on some weeds. I rubbed a few sticks together lighting a fire. By the end it was charred in some parts and raw in others.

We picked off the good parts. Though it wasn’t that good anyways. We started making our way to the cliff. I hope I’m not wrong. Or else they could be dead in the next few days. We have to get there fast. At least the hailing stopped. So we decided to stop hugging the tree line. It was noon now. We've been walking for quite a long time now. We would be walking faster if we were not injured. I'm sure it will take the rest of the day to walk there. Even more if we take a lot more time to break.

Just thinking about how long the journey would take made my mind throb. It made me think back to an easier, simpler time. Sixteen years ago when I was eight. I was an energetic little boy. Running through the outskirts of the forest. One day I found a flower field. After that I was never able to find it again. If only I knew 2 years later I would be taken away from my family. To train to fight.

I was only ten years old. It was a rainy day that one fateful moment. It was raining outside. Lots of mud puddles all around me. Rain crashing down all around. My mother, just nitting in the background. When a soldier in armor much like what we have today. Just not as up to date. He grabbed onto my arm walking me away. My mother didn't even try to stop him.

A few years later I learned that my mother signed me up for it. But back then they needed lots of soldiers. Ever since the N.G.C's started their uprising. I went through vigorous training that I didn't want to do. Only because my mother traded me in for a quick buck. Though she died a few years later from an overdose. Probably got the drugs from the money she sold me away from.

During the training they showed me the N.G.C's tactics and how ruthless they really are. That's how I know they are the enemy. I have devoted my life to stopping them. They are almost as bad as the Zepher's. It has been rumored that the Zepher's brainwashed the citizens to support their cause. The wrong cause.

I remember the first time I saw the plasma sword. Seeing the bright red handle with a gold insert. I felt it was too bright. But there are some variants to be more camouflaged. Not to mention the bright cyan blade. It had an interesting design. It's not really a complete blade. It doesn't need to be because the modified plasma blade is too hot. Though I like the design. A rectangle out on the blade side, and a small portion out inside the blade in the shape of a triangle. Now don't get me started on the practice blade, you have to train with.

The bright silver blade. That gets engulfed in cyan when you ignite it. When not touching it shuts off. Just in case you drop it. I cut off my teacher's finger from it slipping out of my hand. It would have been the whole hand if it wasn't a training one. After that he wasn't a teacher any more. If you don't have a pointer finger you can't shoot a gun or ignite a plasma sword.

The teacher after that was a lot meaner. Some of the kids even got whipped. So I tried my best to be as good as possible. The worst thing I got out from him was the bruise on my cheek. Those were a tough twelve years. These last four have been a lot easier. Working with the guns was a lot funner.

I was the top of the class every single year. I hit a bullseye almost every single time. The only person who was above me was Raith. Man he's such a good shot. The mannequins that popped up out of nowhere was my favorite. Though they never changed where they were, so after a while the course became predictable. Kind of like what it's actually like on the battlefield. The N.G.C's never changed their hiding spots.

The best part is the courses. The indoor ones seemed more manufactured. With a whole lot of plastic. So many bullet holes within it. We used rubber bullets in those courses in case anybody gets hit. I got a black eye from one of those. You had to climb up walls by the cracks in the slanted wall. Squeezing in between walls to get from place to place. Jumping down dozens of feet.

Robots that you had to shoot rubber bullets into slots so they stopped firing back. Always had to get into weird places. Places where they won't be able to see you. Places where they can't fire back at you. One of my favorite spots to hide was in a tiny crawl space underneath all the buildings. At one point I hid right in front of the barricade. That was an easy one to take down. No matter how painful those years were, they were really fun. But my favorite part of the training was the outdoor courses.

We mainly did them during the rain. But we did do it sometimes when it was dry. We used just dummies instead of robots. They would short serket in the rain. We had to crawl under barbed wire attached to wooden beams. You also had to jump through obstacles and slide down roofs. Syless broke his arm on one of those courses.

I know my mother died but I don't know what happened to my father. He left when I was young. One day he just wasn't there. Nobody knows what happened to him. He probably paid a smuggler to sneak him out in one of their ships. Not many people liked him before that. Imagine their reactions when he left.

A lot of people thought my mother sold me away because he left. That she was so depressed she sold me away so I didn't see her turn to drugs. Anyways, I guess I spaced out for only an hour. I only snapped out of the trance because Seth poked at me.

"Dude can we take a break," said Seth. "We've been walking for a while now."

We sat down behind some rocks to get cover. Just in case anybody shoots at us. Seth's a traitor to both the U.G.C and the N.G.C. I am also considered a traitor because I'm helping Seth. I should have killed him while I had the chance. I should have killed all the other N.G.C's too when I had the chance. Though it got me thinking what would have happened.

We walked up the stairs staring down the N.G.C's. Dray on guard and Syless right behind him just in case. Raith pointing just in case. I lift my rifle and aim it right at

Seth's face. Pulling down on the tight trigger. Let it release like a rope snapping. With a slight hum and vibration.

The plasma beam crashing into Seth's face. It disintegrates with an explosion of blood splattering everywhere. His lifeless body crashing to the ground. With his helmet rolling on it. Filled with Seth's very own blood.

The ones in robes point their guns at us. The ones in the armor turned at me and did the same. I see Dray look at me with a seriously look. We then go flying from an explosion. I land on my back, Syless, and Dray land on their sides. I look over and see Raith missing the bottom half of him. I see two of the armored ones executing Dray.

I fire at the both of them landing each shot in their heads. I continue to fire at the other ones. But I only manage to kill a few more. Syless goes running and I try to do the same. But I just couldn't move. Right then I realised I was paralyzed. One in armor walked up to me holding a stone. He dropped it on my head causing it to go splat.

Syless was running through the forest before he made a stop at a temple. He's completely out of breath. A beam from a robed one crashed into the temple as Syless ducked away. His right arm was blown off. He retreated into the temple with more beams crashing into it. He hid behind a pillar in the corner of the temple.

A whole wall came crashing down. The pillar he was hiding behind fell on his leg. He couldn't move anywhere. One of the robed ones picked up the exposed ax from the wall. Clutching on to it with both hands and he was walking towards Syless.

He swung the heavy thing at Syless. It smacked into the pillar causing it to fall down. The ax hit into the wall because of the weight of it. The wall fell over smacking the robed one in the head. He fell to the ground, blood spewing from his head. It released the pillar from Syless's leg so he began to run. An armored one swung the ax, hitting Syless's achilles tendon. With one final swipe Syless's head came clean off.

I think it was best I didn't shoot him then. After that we got up and started walking again. We walked for about ten minutes before we noticed something. Up ahead we saw some movement. At first we thought it was an animal. But it was too big to be an animal, and too fast. There are three of them too. Wait, that's Raith, Dray and Syless. Why didn't I think that at first?

I looked around and saw Mortem chasing after them. I ignited the plasma blade and swiped at the tree. It fell on top of Mortem, knocking him down. I cut down a few more to secure him on the ground.

"Run!" I heard one of them scream.

We ran towards them. After a few minutes we managed to catch up. They were actually in better condition than we are. We leaped up and behind a rock. We dug in so we could hide under it. After getting under we pushed dirt up to block the view. With a little peep hole to peek out of.

"That won't hold him for long," said Syless, "we already tried that."

The rock shifted a little bit. He must have jumped onto it. We were as quiet as we could be. We saw Mortem run off. Once he was out of sight we dug our ways out.

"The mountains just up ahead we should head that way," said Raith.

We ran for a few minutes. Until we reached the tunnel to get to the other side of the mountain. It took a few minutes to get through it. But once we got out we took a little break. From there I looked at Raith, Syless, and Dray to access their damage.

Raith seemed in the best condition. Just chipped armor and a few scratches. Though the padding was all torn up. And his poncho was all ripped up. It was a lot shorter with jagged edges. His eye finder was cracked. Oh, an eye finder is a device you attach to your eyes via straps. It allows you to see from far away. Better for aiming instead of using a scope.

Dray wasn't that damaged, but he wasn't in as good a shape as Raith. His left arm was skinned down to the base armor. Even that part was extremely damaged. Other than that he was missing his right boot and had a few scratches. Other than that the armor was pretty clean, except for what I saw was damaged. But Syless was the real problem.

From what I saw he might have internal damage. That really needs to be checked out right away. If not, he probably won't make it. Syless's armor is completely destroyed. All cracked and busted, many holes in it. He doesn't even have a helmet. He is still clinging on, even after what happened.

“What's up with Seth?” asked Syless.

I looked at Seth and noticed he was different. His bright orange hair was turning a dark brown. Only orange near the ends. He also didn't have any freckles. Maybe he was just wearing makeup, did he do that his entire life? I guess he really has been a lie this whole time.

The sun was coming down so we decided to climb up the mountain. We settled near a tree. Right above the tunnel, so when he came out we had a quick escape. We went out and Grabbed a few sticks for a campfire. We used needles from the trees to get the fire going. Syless used his lighter. The fire flared to life, burning Syless's hand a little. He grabbed some medicine out of his bag and dabbed a little bit of cream on it. Afterwards he wrapped it up.

"So how'd you get here?" I asked.

"Well, want to hear a little story?" asked Syless while wrapping up other cuts on his body.

I guess he's going to be telling a story of how they escaped Mortem. He started weaving weeds on his armor. Connecting bits of armor that he had collected. He needed a little more protection.

"Corporals log, star date 2694 eleven days in," said Syless jokinglee.

We all got a laugh out of that one. *BAM!* We heard a tree fall in the distance. It was about a mile away, so we had a few minutes to talk.

"Well let's get started," said Syless. The fire was burning hot, we had to wait a minute so Syless could collect the information.

"Sorry I have a minor concussion," explained Syless.

No wonder why his armor was so damaged. A tree must have fallen on top of him. His back plates were mostly unscaved. Unlike my back. The tree that fell on me, tore that up. My back still aches from it. Good thing I didn't break my back.

"I watched as Dray handed Bly the plasma derringer. I didn't know what it was for, but I didn't think it was going to be a good idea. When he pointed down the derringer I knew he made a mistake. After a minute I figured he got smart and wasn't going to do it. But it flared to life. I clutched my own derringer when I felt a shake and saw a few bricks come down. Fire flared up, Raith's section of the wall falling down, Raith tumbling down with it.

"All of a sudden the ceiling Dray was on top of collapsed sending him to the ground below. I jumped away from the other few explosions watching Bly come down. When a sudden blast knocked me back, hurdling me to the ground. I landed face first in the mud, a stone jabbing me in my side. I got up dizzy, holding my gun and shooting it through a hole in the wall. It just scraped the side of his head. He turned around firing his gun at me. Though the beam hit the wall. The small explosion knocked me back too. One of the bricks hit my head causing my helmet to go off in the distance. Dray came over and helped me get up. He pointed to Raith, so I ran over sticking morphine in his arm from my bag. He jumped up springing to life. He unhooked his eight inch barrel because it was busted. Attaching his much longer barrel. We stepped back into the broken temple, shooting the final few down.

"We watched Bly's and Seth's little duel. We stood there nervous when Seth slit your wrist. Watching the blood slowly trickle down. It touched and nothing happened. We were so relieved. Then the gems slowly started to screw out. Cling, cling, cling, every time a gem fell to the ground. When the final one came undone I flinched.

"Boom! You guys went flying out of there. Both hands clutched each side of the casket. He sat up effortlessly. His crimson eyes glaring at us. He stood up and with a woosh his ax flew into his hand. From there we bolted away. Woosh, I heard from behind me. So I tackled Dray to the ground watching the ax fly ahead of us.

"We laid there as the ax flew back into Mortem's hand. We then got up and darted away. We managed to catch up to Raith. Though he's pretty slow, so it was easy.

We took a small pitstop, out of breath. I lost my derringer so Dray gave me his plasma sword.

"A tree fell in the distance. So I ignited both my plasma swords asl saw Mortem come up in the distance. I chopped the tree causing it to fall. The tip of the tree crashed into Mortem and he barely even flinched. Though he seemed to get stuck in the leaves. He brought his ax up and struck the tree. The whole thing split in two.

"We started to run. Zoom! I heard from behind me. I started to see a large shadow getting closer and closer to me. I stopped and turned around, then Bam!"

'Woah a tree just hit you?" asked Seth.

"Yeah!" said Syless, "It struck my left shoulder. Causing me to land on my back and slide. My poncho ripped from under me. Strangling me for a minute. My heart was pounding. Shrapnel from my armor pierced my chest. Luckily I was towards the end of the tree, so the log on me wasn't as thick. I figured they just went and left me. I jumped with fear when two hands crashed into it. I figured they were Mortem's but they weren't silver. So I sighed with relief. He crouched down with a stressed look on his face. My eyes focused and I noticed it was Raith. He managed to lift it up about a foot.

"I felt someone grab my armpits and dragged me away from the tree. I was a little dizzy but managed to get up. I managed to collect pieces of my armor and packed it in my bag. I grabbed a needle of morphine in my arm. I felt a sweet-sweet rush and my head began to clear. Feeling the sweet buzz of relief. We saw Mortem coming up to us. I was missing one of my plasma swords. So I swiped a few trees. A fire lifted up causing the trees to crash into Mortem. We then began to hide behind trees.

“We each hid behind our own tree. The trees made up a circle. He stood in the center of it. It took a minute to think of a plan. Dray stepped back because he doesn't have a plasma sword. Me and Raith set it to stealth mode. In stealth mode it’s not as loud but not as powerful either. From there we got into stance.

“We both cut one tree that we were near. They tumbled onto Mortem and he only had the chance to strike one. He chopped the one Raith cut, and mine smacked him in the head. While he was off balance we ran to the next tree. This time he swung up on mine. Causing the top to go flying. The rest of the stump fell on his foot. Raiths tree bonked him on his head.

“Running to the next tree we did it as fast as we could. This time both of them hit Mortem. The seven foot giant fell to his knees. We got to the next trees chopping them down. Both bashing them in his head again. We ran to the next trees and the next. The four trees fell on him at once pinning him to the ground. The final trees were the biggest ones. Two times the size of the other ones. They started to slide off, tipping the stump crushing from the weight. Both fell at once. Bam! It sounded, as it crashed into Mortem. Creating a slight fissure. In the surrounding area.

“We knew it wouldn’t take long before he could get out. We started to run when the logs rustled. We got far enough away, so I decided to do a quick medical check. Dray seemed fine with just a few cuts and Raith also only had a few cuts. Me on the other hand I noticed I had a broken rib and a strained ankle. Probably a few bruised ribs.”

"You and Seth don't look in bad shape yourselves," Syless said to me, "I decided to put another morphine shot in my arm. I just always feel so much better after I take one. The relief it brings to me. The sensation of it. The mind numbingly buzz. If I could, I would have a machine in me that pumps that stuff in my bloodstream every minute. I'd give up my arm for that.

"We decided to go towards the cliff. Just in case we had to jump in the water. I grabbed a small stick and wrapped it around my ankle. Didn't want to have it turn into a break. We took a minute to get our ground. Figuring out that we had to go diagonally to the left. At first we were worried we were going to run into Mortem that way.

"But the ax went flying towards us. Though it was far above us because we were on a steep incline. I noticed Mortem jerked his arm. Somehow it made the ax fly down in our direction. Me and Dray leaped out of the way so it didn't hit us. A head of the ax went deep into the mud. But I pulled it out with ease.

"We were running but I was slowed down by how heavy the ax was. Mortem must be really strong considering how easily he maneuvers it. The ax started tugging to the left of me. I looked over and saw Mortem moving his arm. He was trying to get it to fly back to him. It must have a mind of its own.

"I looked down and noticed an eye between both heads of the ax. I freaked out dropping it. Causing it to fly back to Mortem, tripping me. I managed to land in a roll. Turning around shooting at Mortem. The beam hit his chest. Reflected up into his helmet and then down into the ground. His armor must have been made of a crystalized material. It was as shiny as the ax was.

"Throughout the ax's color it was dulled. From the mud and some parts stained with a light red. He must have killed lots of people in the past. I turned around, and started jogging my way as fast as I could. I didn't manage to catch up to them. But I still was about ten feet behind them. My ankle was aching with pain and I wanted to stop. But if I did, Mortem would have killed me.

"I then felt like I stepped on nothing. I looked out and started falling down into a valley. Rolling down my head spinning. My armor is getting slimy from the mud. My foot landed in a mud puddle causing it to twist, before I flew down to the bottom of the valley.

"Good thing the mud bank broke my fall. I rolled around a few times. To make sure he couldn't see me. Slightly moving up the bank. My armor soaking up the mud. I heard a zoom from the ax. Though it was far away so I wasn't worried. I stopped going as fast as I was going. Only in fear the Mortem would spot me and end my life. I stopped when I heard something land in the mud.

"I moved my head over a little while watching Mortem. He picked up the ax and continued going up the valley. Once he disappeared from view I got up. I slowly walked at the bottom of the valley. Just in case I ran into Mortem at the top. After a while I reached the end of the valley. I walked up the steep incline. I took a minute to take my ground. After a minute I heard someone call my name. I turned around and saw Dray and Raith. So I turned around and continued walking when they were a few feet behind me. After a few minutes they caught up.

"It was an hour or two before we ran into Mortem. We

weren't going to if it didn't start hailing. We ended up hiding under a tree. We were dry most of the time. Sometimes a piece of ice managed its way onto us. After about forty minutes Mortem showed up.

"They started running, but I couldn't keep up. After a while the hail stopped. I cut down one more tree in a last ditch effort. He just lifted up his ax slightly. The ax caused the tree to not even hit him. The bottom landed before his feet. The top half almost hit him in the head though.

"He swung his ax into the tree, causing it to go flying. I ducked out of the way. It ended up hitting Dray. It smashed into his shoulder causing him to fall down. Once I got to him I picked him up. He was clutching onto his shoulder. I assessed the damage and determined it wasn't broken. A few minutes after that, I noticed you guys in the corner of my eye. After a few minutes you guys caught up. Then we got under the rock, and after a few minutes I was telling this story."

Once Syless clunkily finished his story we heard stomps in the tunnel. So we put out the fire and got ready to run. I clutched onto my rifle and Seth grabbed two of his final seven knives. Syless and Raith were holding their guns, Dray holding Seth's derringer.

"This is it," whispered Dray.

But out came a bunch of N.G.C's. There are five-five in total. I can't wait to stomp all their heads in. At first they didn't notice us. But Seth threw one of his knives. Landing in the eye of one of them. He fell on his knees, blood streaming down from the wound. Before face planting in the mud. Causing the plasma knife to go through his skull. A little blue from the blade sticking out.

They pointed their guns at us, so we hid behind the trees. Though they wouldn't hold for long. All of a sudden one of Raiths beams went into the skull of another. The jaw fell to the ground as the face melted into a bloody muk, before the head fell off the neck. From there they started shooting at him. He ignited his plasma sword, cutting off part of the tree above him. Causing it to fall on one of them.

With them distracted, I put the bursts of beams into one of them. *Buzz, buzz, buzz. Buzz, buzz,buzz.* My rifle was making, hitting him three at a time. His armor getting scorched and busted. Until he fell onto his back. We heard a clunking noise from the tunnel. This time we knew it was Mortem from the metal sounds.

Seth and Raith unignited their blades. Raith also got down from the tree. We stepped back before we actually saw him. Going out another few feet when he came out of the tunnel. Holding onto the ax, Mortem walked up to the final alive N.G.C who was stuck under the tree. Mortem didn't even care to use his ax. Putting his foot over the N.G.C's grunts face. Rubbing his foot into the grunts' nose. Before putting a little bit of pressure causing his face to explode from the pressure. Creating a blood soup, with little bone bits floating within it. Even the helmet was crushed, I gagged at the sight.

Raith stepped on a stick, causing it to snap. Mortem looked over at us, pointing his ax in our direction. Throwing it with one hand. I jumped out of the way. The ax going far in the distance. It flew back towards my legs. I jumped over the ax coming at me. Bouncing off my arms onto my feet. I hurt my forearms in that stunt.
"Run!" screamed Dray.

We started running as fast as we could. We decided to stay on the mountain slope. If we went down to the fields, Mortem could get us easily. Up here we have the trees blocking the way. The ax came back, but way above us. I think Mortem's plan was to drop trees on us. Even though we were moving too quickly for the trees to fall on us.

A tree fell in the distance, sitting diagonal propped up by the tree it was sitting on. All the people who were ahead of me. Actually everybody but Syless was ahead of me, went around it. But I got distracted checking to see if Syless was okay. By the time I looked forward the tree was right there. So I put my hands on it to propel myself up. Going over the tree part. I twisted both my forearms again while landing on my feet.

I stopped turning back to Syless. Limping his way towards us. The ax landed right in front of Syless and he tripped over it. Landing on his face, I and Syless looked over at the same time seeing Mortem leap into the small woods in front of Syless. I shot my plasma rifle at him right away, I'm not going to lose my friend now.

Syless swung the ax at Mortems head. It ended up hitting the bottom of Mortems left horn. The armor and bits of the ax flew off and the horn got a little crushed. Syless brought up the ax at an angle. Adding more damage to the armor and causing the horn to fall off. It klanked on Mortems foot causing him to look down at it. Mortem slammed the bottom of his fist into Syless's jaw. Syless fell back holding his jaw. Mortem picked up the ax and swung at me. It landed into the stump of the tree causing it to split.

I noticed Syless started running off. I think Mortem noticed too, probably because I was looking at him. Mortem turned over and threw his ax at him. Once I noticed he missed, I ran. *Zoom* I heard behind me. *Zoom* I heard again, coming from behind me. I jumped and rolled watching the ax going past me. *That was close* I thought.

I saw it coming towards me, so I leaped out of the way, causing it to go behind me. After a few more minutes I reached the field. I saw the others ahead of me again. Though they were much farther ahead of me. After looking at them I thought about Syless. I turned around and saw him just coming out of the forest.

“Come on!” I yelled.

I looked forward and noticed the others were all ducked down. I ended up getting to them, ducking down as well. Up ahead was a group of eight N.G.C’s. I realised Seth wasn’t with us, so I looked over and saw he was getting closer to them. Seth jumped on one of their backs and slit his throat. The N.G.C’s started shooting at him, so he used the dead body as a shield.

Then we started shooting at them. Two more fell to the ground, from the array of our plasma beams. I looked back and saw Syless coming. He made it to us, igniting his plasma sword. Then threw it like a spear. It ended up piercing one of the grunts' shoulders. Seth then grabbed onto the plasma sword bringing it down, causing the grunts arm to fall off. Then he stabbed that grunt in the face. The grunt fell back with the plasma sword still stuck in his face.

Raith shot one of them through the throat. The grunt clutched his throat and started shooting at us. But Seth grabbed onto him and turned him around. The grunt ended up shooting one in the eye. After that Seth snapped his neck. He threw one of his plasma knives. It ended up going through the middle of a grunts face. The grunt fell on his side, blood streaming from his face.

The final grunt shot at us, the beam going through Dray's shoulder pad. The grey protective padding underneath got singed. All of us shot at him. He got pushed back by every beam that hit him. Eventually falling over, a minute after that he bled to death.

"We gotta get going," said Dray.

Dray helped Syless get up and we started walking. After Syless was moving well, Dray went back and picked up the plasma sword and knife from the dead bodys. He caught up with us quickly because we were all walking. After a minute of walking we got to the forest on the other side of the valley.

There were lots of pine needles on the forest floor. I guess that's because of all the pine trees in the forest. There's mainly pine trees brought over from Earth. The other tree brought over from Earth is the oak tree. A few other trees localized to this planet were classified as the Cornus tree and the Desher tree.

Zoom! All of a sudden the ax went past us. Before flying back into Mortem's hand. He swung his ax, cutting down two trees. I ignited my plasma sword and Dray ignited the sword and knife. Seth took Raiths plasma sword and ignited it. Raith and Syless pointed their guns at him.

We were all walking backwards as he was walking towards us. Only one of us looked back at a time to make sure none of us tripped.

Here we go, I thought. Mortem stopped walking towards us and we stopped walking backwards. Mortem was glaring at us and we were glaring at him. Oh I was nervous, so nervous I felt the sweat go down my brow. I started to hyperventilate. We couldn't stop him, the only way we could is if we got his ax. That's the only thing that seems to do damage to him. If only there was something else made of the same material. Our plasma swords don't seem to do anything. Only scorches his armor slightly, maybe if we stood there long enough it could burn a hole through. But there's no way we'd be able to know.

"I wish I didn't come," said Dray.

"I wish I didn't either," I responded.

Part: 3

The Astral Plane

Soldier's log number six, star date 2694 nine days in. Commander Ora just brought me and Zach to the training center in the military building. I got a little nervous being in there, but I guess that's my fault. She brought us over to the back room. There's a forty inch holographic television. This room is also filled with other holographic projectors. The windows were very tinted for some reason. Probably because of the holograms.

It wasn't a very big room, only fifteen by eighteen. It had black padded walls, with a dark blue padded double triangle on the floor. The rest of the padded floor was a deep crimson. There was a closet in one of the fifteen foot walls. Ora opened it up and grabbed something from within it. It was three cushions. She set the three cushions down. Two of them at the end points of the triangle, and one at a point where the two triangles meet. They were a dark royal blue, with four golden tassels at each corner. It had a bunch of golden swirly patterns that branch out of the U.G.C insignia. I was a little curious, so I flipped it over. Though there was nothing on that side. I don't know why she made us sit on the cushions, when the floor is padded.

"Von, Zach, so glad that you guys decided to do this," said Ora.

What is this, a seminar? Do I have to talk? I don't want to talk.

"You guys only need to talk a little, I'll be doing most of the talking," said Ora.

Yay! I have to talk. Though I guess I don't have to talk too much. I don't like talking. Kind of ironic, considering I talk into this tape recorder all the time. Though usually not around people. I mainly do it after the events. Imagine being in the middle of the battlefield and recapping the events as they happen. *I just picked up my sniper rifle with one hand and shot a guy in the face! Oh-no somebody just shot me in my chest, I'm bleeding to death!*

"I'm here to teach you guys about something," said Ora, "It's called the Astral plane."

Astral plane? Does this have to do with the stars? And if so, what about them? There must be some kind of connection. Maybe it's not just about the stars. Maybe there's something more. I'd probably have more information if I would just let her talk.

"You've always mentioned it, I'm surprised you're actually teaching it," said Zach.

So he has mentioned this before. Probably before I came here. I wonder what he's said about it before. Probably not too much, then everybody would know about it. Why would he decide to teach me? How does he know I'm trustable enough to tell me? How does he know if I'm not a spy? He's putting a lot of weight on my shoulders. I hope I don't go and blurt it out.

"It's, well, very hard to explain what it actually is," said Ora.

Great, this is going to be long. There's probably several long sessions. I hope this is worth it, otherwise I'd just stop coming.

"It can only be activated once you let everything go," said Ora, "Now imagine-

"You stop focusing, but stay extremely focused on one certain thing. Everything you know has been dropped. Life and death become one being. The colors of everything disappear. Except for yourself and the one thing you're focusing on. The white stars above you glow against the dark black sky. You have a feeling within you, that can only be described as being in another dimension! Almost as if you are freely floating through space."

I don't think I would really like that. It'd make me feel like a ghost, where I'm not welcome to the world. Though a lot of people might like the feeling. Being free from all constrictions. Feel nothing as stuff passes by you. But you can only focus on two things. Yourself and the one other thing that you focus on, whatever it may be. Some people would find it free, but I would find it more constricting to only be able to focus on two things.

"You can pass through the soul thing you are focusing on. Almost as if you're a ghost. You get a slight tingling feeling passing through them. I wouldn't know, but I'm pretty sure the person you're passing through can feel it too."

"Wouldn't you end up passing through your clothes?" asked Zach.

Ora responded, "only if you focus on them."

We all chuckled at that. It wasn't very funny.

"But, how exactly do we activate this?" I asked.

Zach continued, "yeah, how do you think, but not think at the same time?"

"Well that's not quite right, maybe I should elaborate. You don't think it, you feel it. You feel the empty plane. You feel all the stars above you. There power emanates on to you. Allowing the power to flow through your veins. The light of the stars blinding you. You feel as if you can kill something with one punch. Everything around you slows down at a superhuman pace. So much that you can almost sense their moves before they do them."

"About being able to phase through something," said Zach, "what if you were to get out of the astral plane, while phasing through something?"

"While phasing through something and suddenly popping out, it would go through you. It would split you apart. If a wall is partly hollow the part of yourself that was phasing through those parts would be in those parts."

"What if a sword halfway phased through someone," I asked. The sword would be embedded into the person. Sure there would be a little bit of blood. It would be easier to pull it out because there's already a hole from the sword. Unless it's an oddly shaped sword with small serrated edges across the blade. Then it would be slightly harder to pull it out because it's not one big hole in them."

"How would it be harder to pull it out, if there's more surface area of the blade?"asked Zach.

"Well if there's three within the body with two inches in between them, you'd have to cut all the flesh in between. Oh, on the topic of phasing, if you're going to phase, never focus on the ground. Though there are some exceptions. Like if you're in a building. But if you're phasing through the floors, be aware of what floor you're on. Otherwise just like if you were on the ground, you'd keep going down until you reached the core of Valor."

"What if you stopped phasing halfway into the ground?" I asked.

"Just like what would happen if you did that with the wall. Whatever part of yourself occupying the part of the wall, stone, or dirt would get stuck in it. While whatever part of yourself that isn't occupying that, would come clean off, falling into whatever clear empty space. Poor Wess, he died that way. Him and Bly were the last two people, I tried to teach before you two. But I cut it short, when Wess went through the floor, to his own death.

That's why I haven't teached this in these long two years, and that's why Bly became the captain. It was hard because Wess was the first one to join the team. It didn't affect Bly as much because he had just started a few days before. I never realised the similarities, please give me a minute as I find some alcohol to drink."

I wonder what that's about? It's not like that for her to run out. Though I've only known him for a day, so what do I even know? Maybe there's a small similarity between me and Bly, it wouldn't be very interesting if we were both the same, so I find that very unlikely. I just want to know where he went.

"This is going to be fun," chirped Zach.

Since Zach said that, I can't wait to see how Ora acts drunk. Must be pretty fun considering that reaction. If she's even getting alcohol, it's a pretty rash reaction since I just said I didn't know where she went. Maybe she just went to get a coffee, or just to kill herself. We really just have to wait and see what she's going to do. Anyway, she's back.

We sat there for a while not saying anything. I didn't because I was focusing on Ora's cocktail. The bright lime green, which is in contrast to the bright cyan cocktail from Rozz. Not like there's different kinds of alcohol. It was in a tall clear glass, a kind of steam seeping down the cup. It had a few ice balls and a striped red and white straw.

Ora Spoke, "so-uh, it's really easy to block punches I guess. In fast hand to hand to foot to foot combat. If you are skilled enough with the astral plane, it would be very easy to quickly block the punches. Like if you caught their foot and uppercutted them, then as they go to punch you back you can jump into the astral plane. From there you can phase through them to their other side. Then you can punch him in the back of their neck!"

At least she's going to have a few good points while she's drunk. Though she's definitely not going to be as knowledgeable. I hope he got through all the big points, at least she's teaching us in what way to use it. I can't wait to hear all the good points she's going to teach us. I wonder how crazy it's going to get.

"When he turns around to punch you back, phase through him again. Then push him over, and kick him till he's dead! Unless you have a weapon, then you can phase through him and kill 'em. Or while phasing before you leave the astral plane keeps the blade inside. So when you do pop out, you can kill him on the spot."

Right now she's just kind of reiterating himself. Maybe that's a good thing. Maybe there's nothing else to talk about. Or if there is, she'll get there eventually. But I guess we don't know. She did say it was a three day lesson. Bly must have stopped during the second lesson, considering Wess died practicing it. I have a good idea on the first and second lesson, I wonder what the third one's like. Maybe actually using it in battle! That would be super cool. I wonder what it is like using it in battle?

"Hello?" asked Zach, poking me.

"Yeah you've been out for a while," continued Ora.

Zach responded, " it's only been five minutes."

"Sorry, just where can I get one of those?" I responded.

From there we got up and left the room. We took the elevator to the first floor and left the building. We went to the building one behind us. It's in contrast to the one in front of us, which had a library instead of a bar. We walked through the door and to the right into another door. There were flashing lights. Pink and green spotlights going all over the

place. A quartet of singers singing a song.
"Mee kee see bee nee koratta," they sang non stop.

We went to the bar and sat down.
I said, "I'd like one of what she's got."

I said that and Ora held up her drink.
Zach said, "I'd like one too."

After two minutes he presented us with our drinks. We got up and left after that. We left and made our way back to the training room. We sat down on the cushions and I took my first sip of the cocktail. A buzzing sensation went throughout my body. I can see why Zach was so excited. The rest of the night is going to be fun! My head still hurts from that night. Though it's still pretty fuzzy, I can still recall it. It was only a few days ago.

Ora said, "so I lied, kinda. While within the astral plane you can see into the past and future. Regularly you can see a few seconds into the future. But if you go to an enchanted spot, like a temple or cemetery. You can look back or forward in time. You will be able to see everything that happened and everything that will. I didn't tell you guys because you can use this power to change your future. So if you know your future you could avoid it. You may say you can just stay in the astral plane, but you can get stuck in it.

"I know what you're thinking, how can you get stuck? Well if you stay in it for too long, you will be trapped. Almost as if you had forgotten how to get out. After that, these flying demon things will chase after you, and the only way to get out is for someone to find you within the astral plane. But you'll be dead before then."
"What about seeing into the past and future?" asked Zach.

"Well when you get to one of those spiritual spots, a

bubble will pop up. Moving the bubble towards the left, it shows you the future, and when you move it to the right it shows your past. All the other people that have gone into the astral plane that I met, and who found these don't understand why it's like this. Most of them thought it was a gift from the gods."

"What do you mean bubble?" I asked.

"It's a floating circle two feet above the ground. When you push it to either side the first circle goes away and another one pops up. It has a moving image of an important event that happens, and you can expand or shrink it. Depending on how much you want to see it."

"So, It's more of just a floating circle than actually a sphere?" asked Zach.

"Huh?" responded Ora.

Zach sounded too intelligent to be drunk. I looked over and saw he hadn't even drinken a sip of his cocktail. When I first met Zach I didn't think he was smart. He just seemed like a guard. A brawn in a team of just brains. But no, he's just as smart as the rest of them. He just didn't seem like he would be that way. I guess that means you really can't judge a book by its cover.

"So-uh yeah I guess it is just a floating sphere," said Ora, "Instead of a bubble thing,"

"What about those demon things?" I asked.

"Well they're the typical demon. Except that they're all bone with little bits of flesh on them in some places. Their bottom halves are missing, and they have a cloak. The cloak is tattered and ripped, there are holes on the back for their bone wings. They have lime green eyes, their bones are a dark red and their dead skin a dark blue."

"Oh-oh-oh," shouted Ora.

"If you're in a dark moral terror, you can see dead people. More specifically people you know. If one of your friends dies and something bad happens to you, nothing specific, it could've been your friend's death. They will appear in the last state you saw them. The only way to get rid of them is to let go and let them be free."

"What do you mean by let go?" I asked Ora, "and let them be free?"

"To let go, you need to be at your inner peace, with the situation. If you're extremely upset about or worried, or even stressed it won't work. If you find peace, they can let go. Letting go means they can go on to the after life. To finally be at rest, and only you have the control to allow them to move on. If you can't find peace, they can't move on."

"What happens if you don't move on?" I asked.

"They hang around, watching your every move. Waiting until they can leave, and it's not by choice that they stay with you. They have too, because you are the one that is holding them back. Their dead bodies will follow you everywhere you go."

That sounds terrible, I would hate for that to happen to me. Dead people following you around, just because you haven't let go of them. I just couldn't imagine what that would be like. I just hope that doesn't happen to me. With it being my friends too. Just your dead friends everywhere you go. Sounds terrible.

"What if you die before accepting that they're gone?" asked Zach, "Will they get to the afterlife?"

"Or just stay in the Outer World?" I asked.

"Well, if you die, I don't think their spirits will go on. They'll just sit around to haunt the outer world. Never able to move on for an eternity. Of just being a ghost, no one can

see you, no one can hear you. No one can feel you, no one knows that you're there. It's just sad to think about it. Just not
able to do anything but watch, not able to do anything."

"Though that's just a theory, maybe they are able to move on once the person dies. It's just hard to know if it is true. Only because you'd have to die to get the results, and you can't talk to a dead person. Well you can, but you can't if you haven't met the requirements to do so."

"Wait? So you can talk to them?" I asked Ora.

"Yes, you can talk to them. But if you talk to them in a public place, everybody will think you're crazy. Only because you're talking to no one. So if you do it in a private place, nobody thinks you're crazy. You can only talk to them because of the astral plane."

"So you can communicate through the astral plane?" asked Zach.

"Yes, you can communicate through the astral plane. Though I don't know how or why. It can be a multitude of things, personally I think it makes us psychic. Though not to the extent to be able to read each other's minds. But just enough to talk through it. It would be good for battle. You can have many reactions with teammates in the astral plane, even if they're not teammates."

Wow this brings a new light to the astral plane. If you're in it and near other people you are just able to communicate with them. I can't stop thinking of the strategies and changing the strategies while in the astral plane. Just the things you can do with this. So many new opportunities. Maybe that's the third lesson! To communicate within the astral plane. Maybe communicate while in combat. Oh, I'm so excited to see what it is. I hope it's something cool like that, it would be stupid if it was something like morality.

Zach asked, “Can you do anything else inside the astral plane?”

“Yeah! Can you like to fight people in the astral plane?” I asked, “maybe like an enemy, or like training?”

“Yes, you can fight in the astral plane. You’d be pretty capable of using the astral plane as a weapon. Though if both of you were to use it that way, the fight could get pretty long. But not many people know how to use the astral plane so it usually doesn't happen. Besides, most people that know about the astral plane are allies.”

“Well, what about fighting in it?” asked Zach.

“Well, the astral plane is a different plane of existence. So you can fight each other. Though, you’d both have to be focusing on each other. So it would be virtually impossible to fight inside the astral plane. But you can still use it, popping in and out of the astral plane. I think I covered everything you guys need to know about the astral plane. It’s starting to become night, so I’m ending this lesson today. We’ll do more tomorrow, trying to get into the astral plane.”

She then downed the rest of the cocktail and stumbled off. Waddling his way out, hitting his shoulder on the door frame. After that me and Zach walked out together. Putting our cocktails into a trash can. We had to wait a minute to go into the elevator because Ora just took it.

“Excited for tomorrow?” I asked.

Zach responded, “kinda, are you?”

“A little bit,” I said nonchalantly even though I was excited.

The elevator came back and we stepped in once the

two people inside stepped out. We didn't say anything at all after that. We got out of the elevator and walked down the hallway. Walking into the room and it just felt empty. The only one in there was Ora. The others must still be on the mission. Ora was drooling out of her mouth snoring. So me and Zach mutually decided to hit the hay. We turned off the light and laid down.

Right after that we heard a loud noise in the distance. I hope the team is okay. That was probably them, It's probably gonna get them in trouble. But I decided not to worry about it because I'd be up all night. Just thinking about bad things that could have happened.

I woke up to a nurse, poking my arm. With a slight headache and blurred vision. It took me a minute to sit up straight. It must have been the cocktail, though I only drank half of it. The drink must have had a high alcohol content. "Time to check on Cuchillo in the bloodstream," she said.

I got up and stumbled my way to the government building, with the nurse accompanying me. We made our way to my room, and I laid down on my bed. She stuck a few IVs in my right arm. She put a needle a little higher into my arm. Probably to check my blood alcohol, or Cuchillo. After a few minutes the doctor came in. Why didn't they use the tubes?

"Had an old Dem-Wise huh?" asked the doctor.

But I just layed there confused. I know that's Ora's last name, but what does it have to do with me being drunk?

"It's Ora's special cocktail she made himself," said the doctor, "after that they put it on the menu."

Well I guess that clears it up a little bit.

"Almost the rest of the Cuchillo was sucked to the metal," said the doctor, "except for a little bit, but all of that was

killed off by the Dem-Wise."
"So, what does that mean?" I asked.
The doctor replied, "we're taking the metal out."

Him and two other people brought me to the surgical room and put me under. Though they didn't knock me out, because the procedure isn't that bad. So I could slightly feel it and see out. Though my vision was blocked because of the mask. I felt the smooth delicate cut, lengthwise across my arm. With clamps pulling my skin back. I started seeing little visions of the nut man again. He wasn't as disturbing this time. Just doing his regular singing-dancing routine. Sometimes a nice tip of a fedora at the end. He went away when I jerked because they started pulling it out of my arm. One doctor held me down because of it. A sharp pain was surging through my left arm. All of a sudden it was gone and I was relieved. Out of the corner of my eye I saw a blood-stained piece of metal, with a bunch of brown blotches on it. After that I blacked out. I woke up, with the doctor standing there.
"The surgery's finished, you're free to go!" said the doctor.

After that I got a good look at the time. It was eight in the morning! So I got up and put on my jacket. But while putting on my jacket, I noticed my wrapped arm. I'm glad I don't have to worry about that any more. That song came back to me as I was leaving.

The airs just fine
In the evening
But the pain's not leaving
So I joined the army
But that wasn't very long

'Cause I got gunned down
But now, I 'll finally be free
'Cause I'll finally be with you again.

The next part came to me! Man, it just came to me. It took me so long to get the last one. This just came to me like that! I made it outside and decided to walk to that meadow. I walked at the edge of the woods for a bit. After a few minutes I made it to the meadow. The flowers looked very good. But they were starting to wilt, probably because it was changing seasons. I ventured further into the meadow and found a little pond. No fish in it though. There was a little stool near it so I decided to sit down. Smelling the perfumes of the flowers around me. Taking in nature, though I decided to stop breathing it in because it was giving me a headache. I then saw someone walking towards me.

"Hi, I'm Von!" I shouted.

She replied, "Yeah, and I'm Elaine.

Oh it's that one girl, she was here the last time I came.

"I think we've done this before," I said.

She shook her head yes in response. I picked a handful of flowers and handed them to her.

"Doing better than last time," Elaine said.

"Well," I said, "I hit my head around that time, and the doctor said that if it got worse I had to see him."

She didn't seem to believe my lie. Though how could I tell her my wife died. It's way too soon, only like my third time seeing her and we're not even in a relationship. But it's too soon for me to start dating again. It hasn't even been a year yet. I can't see myself starting to date again any time soon. After a minute I started to rub my head, to make it seem like I still kinda had a headache. Though it made her more suspicious of my fake injury, so I stopped. You'd think that would make it more believable, I would have thought of it that way.

"You know I'm a nurse," Elaine said, "I have access to all your files." Stalker.

Well I guess that explains why she didn't believe me. But how would she have access to my files if she's only a nurse. I don't know, maybe they have access to that kind of stuff. I looked at her suspiciously, just in case she isn't actually a nurse. But she took a piece of paper out of her brown chesterfield coat and presented it to me. It was an education degree, though technically she's a pharmacist. So she probably had access to my files to recommend the medicine.

"Technically you're a pharmacist, not a nurse," I blurted out.

"Yeah," she said, "and what exactly do you do?"

So I responded, "Well, I used to be a gatekeeper."

She was looking at me confused, so I decided to explain.

"On the planet Rozz there are five towns, and to get through each town you need a ticket," I explained, "So I stand at the gate in between five and four, checking to see if the people have their tickets." Elaine began to say something, but I cut her off. "The reason why there are guards is because the tickets are so expensive, because of that people try to get to other towns without paying anything."

"Why is that important?" asked Elaine.

"Well, because there's a class system, that depends on which town you live in," I responded, "The first town is the wealthiest, everything there is fancy and expensive, but that's only because that's where the government resides." I decided to sit down and kept explaining. "Two and three are around the same wealth wise, but what they do is different. Two creates and builds weapons for the soldiers and guards, While three makes all the food."

"What do you mean wealth and money?" asked Elaine.

"Well people do their jobs and they trade it in for stuff, for three and four the stuff they make can be traded in for more, ergo more wealthy." I explained.

"Next is four, this is where the wealth goes way down," I told Elaine, "They distribute manure to the third town, so three's plants can grow, you can imagine that doesn't give them much wealth."

"What about five?" asked Elaine.

"Five is a little less wealthy because they mine gold, sure it sounds expensive, but not when there's that much," Elaine seemed a little confused about it, "We mainly mine the gold to go to two, for the weapons and one for the town to look nice."

Good, I've seemed to have told her everything about where I came from. Without mentioning the fact that I came here because my wife had died. It's good to steer clear of that for as long as I can. Don't want to show her any of my baggage, especially since we are not going anywhere.

We sat there for hours, saying nothing. Until it started hailing, I checked the time and it was already twelve, so we decided to leave. Besides, the lesson starts at twelve-fifteen anyways. We both went in different directions, though I'm pretty sure she is wrong.

At twelve'o'eight I checked the time, because I made it at an old shanty bridge. I have no idea where this is, but it does go across dry land. But it goes very far down. I decided to turn back because I went the wrong way. But I'm pretty sure I went the right way. So I ended up going back at an angle. I ended up at a river, so I walked along it until I found a bridge. It was just like the one near the old temple that Syless had pointed out to me. But it wasn't as broken apart. So I must be just up the river. I put my first foot on a board and it fell. So I sprinted across it until about half-way. The board fell before I reached it and I fell into almost all of the other boards.

I saw a few in front of me fall but one didn't so I clutched onto it as I watched all the other boards besides one other fall. I swung down below the board I was hanging on. My arm hurt because the corner of the board was jabbing into my elbow. I ended up hitting my knee into something, causing the board to shift.

I realised that the two boards still standing were held up by supports. I also noticed that there was enough distance for me to push it over into the other side. I grabbed onto the other side with my left arm and started swinging. Kicking the beam each time. After five times it started falling, but I accidentally swung back again. I let go with one hand and grabbed onto the other board attached to the beam that still works.

I started pushing myself over. But I kicked the other beam causing me to go the other way. My elbow and face hit into the dirt. I stuck my fingers into the ground pulling myself up. I got back up to the top, Only a little injured. It was twelve-twelve so I decided to rush back. I don't want to be late.

I ran through the forest, as the hail crashed down on me. I put my jacket up over my head, to protect it from ice balls crashing down on my head. By twelve-fifteen I made it back to the base, or whatever it's called. So I was only a few minutes late. Ora and Zach didn't seem to mind. Though Ora was definitely in a hangover.

The three of us sat in our seats from yesterday. I couldn't help but see the similarities between the song and me. Which got me thinking how my life has been like the song. Why can't I get it out of my head and I only have one more verse to go. So I started running it in my head.

When the wind blows
Deep at night
Sitting by the fire
Warmness on my feet
Before the wind dies down
But at least I still
Have you besides me

It's almost as if it's a standard evening, but how does it compare to me?

When the wind blows
Deep at night
The fires gone out
I then grew cold
But at least I still
have you besides of me

Two's almost a continuation of the first one.

When the wind blows
Deep at night
The days almost near
The winds gone down
But you're still beside me

Still a continuation, but it's more of an ending. Or really like a new day.

The winds gone out
The sun is rising
Day's finally here
But before I knew it
You were no longer
Besides me

This is where the song really changes, almost as if it was the turning point.

The air is steady
In the mid-day
A drop of rain comes down
Sending chills down my spine
The sad thing is that
You're not besides me

This shows how the last verse happened. The rain symbolizes how this character is feeling. Showing the sadness of the situation, not to mention the chill. That is just terrifying.

The air stands still
In the afternoon
I went to get my jacket
'Cause the rains pouring down
This rain just shows how i'm feeling
I'm cold and
The sad thing is that
You're not besides me

It just kind of proves my last statement, with the whole how I'm feeling part.

The airs just fine
In the evening
But the pain's not leaving
So I joined the army
But that wasn't very long
'Cause I got gunned down
But now, I 'll finally be free
'Cause I'll finally be with you again.

This is where I started to see the similarities. With the whole joining the army part. But the character within this joined the army by choice. I was forced into this, I was happy just being a gate-keeper.

"Von, Von!" I heard Ora shout.

I slowly got a response out, but it was only a "huh?"

“Did you hear anything Ora said?’ asked Zach, “You were zoned out, huh.”

It sounded sarcastic, though I’m pretty sure the “huh” was a joke. Though it doesn't matter.

“She said something?” I asked.

“Oh it’s not that big of a deal,” said Ora, “It was only an introductory thing.”

She motioned for us to stand up and did deep breath motions. So me and Zach did the same.

“No-no you don’t have to do this,” said Ora, “Now watch!”

Just then she turned translucent. You could see right through her, but she’s still there. I swiped at her and my arm went right through her. I did it a few more times and nothing. She chuckled and just walked through the wall. I felt the wall and it wasn’t fake.

“Boo!” I heard Ora scream from behind.

I jumped from her cold finger touching me. Her arm was extremely cold. She pulled her arm back really fast. I guess it was pretty weird that I was doing that.

“Wow, you’re super cold!” I said.

Ora responded chattering, “Yeah that is a slight problem, but it’s not bad when you get used to it.”

“Yeah, you seem very used to that,” said Zach sarcastically.

I responded, “Zach, why are you acting like Syless?”

“Well, somebody has to be the butthead!” joked Zach.

I turned back around to look at Ora and she had disappeared. I felt something so I looked down and I saw her translucent arms going through my chest. I stepped out to be safe.

“Dude, be careful!” I told her.

She just laughed about it. Well I guess she’s not really the serious type. I think she’s trying to show an example of what you can do. She popped out of the astral plane and picked up a sword before going back in. She swung at my head with it. Nothing happened, though I guess you didn't need to know that. She walked to the punching bag in the corner putting her sword into it. She popped out and we watched how the sword was stuck in it. She swung the sword and the punching bag fell, tons of the little beans spilled out. It was so cool how the sword got stuck in it without stabbing it. When you're in the astral plane the laws of physics disappear. hHe went to punch Zach, causing him to flinch, but he went into the astral plane before he hit.

I can't wait to try this out myself. Ora then walked through Zach, popping out after she went all the way through him. Then she tripped Zach causing him to fall over. He turned onto his back, clutching his nose. He sat up putting his hand on his head from dizziness. I looked at Zach's nose and there was blood seeping out of a nostril.

We decided to get a nurse. Thankfully there was one in the other room. The nurses were stationed there. They were only there because of my little accident a few days ago. I wonder if they have shifts. The nurse put a flashlight up to his eyes to see if anything was okay.

"It's just a bloody nose," said the nurse, "Probably from a fall."

Isn't that a good guess.

"Or maybe from the heat?" said the nurse.

So I asked, "isn't getting colder?'

"No, heat from the vents," replied the nurse.

Heat from the vents? There's no vents on Rozz. In the summer it's super hot, and in the winter it gets super cold. Though autumn and spring don't exist on Rozz. At least there's time for you to ease into the weather. But on

Rozz it just starts freezing all of a sudden. The gatekeeper armor doesn't help. The padding makes you overheat in the summer because there is so much of it. In the winter you freeze because there isn't enough padding. That's kinda ironic, isn't it? No, it's not.

She gave him a tissue, and he stuck it in his nose to stop the bleeding. We proceeded to walk to the other room to continue the lesson. We sat back down on the cushions, staring at each other for a good minute.

"Welp, guess I'm not doing that again," weeped Ora.

"You know what Zach," said Ora, "you go first."

Zach responded, "Okay."

"Now let go!" told Ora in a spooky voice.

Zach scrunched up his face, closing his eyes. He opened up his eyes, looking around in surprise. Looking at his hands.

"Woah," said Zach, "am I doing it?"

He was looking around and got in a running stance. He then began to sprint to the wall. Ora lifted up her finger, trying to tell Zach he wasn't in the astral plane. Zach then ran into the tv attached to the wall. He fell onto his back clutching his head. I looked at the TV with a big smashed part in it. With a giant crack going all across it.

"I tried to warn you," said Ora.

Me and Ora started chuckling, but Zach shot us a look so we stopped.

"You're still supposed to focus on something," said Ora.

"Okay," responded Zach, "okay."

He was staring at me, focusing immensely. He started walking towards me waving his arms. Once he got close I covered my eyes so he wouldn't poke them out. He ended up slapping me a few times before he realised he wasn't in the astral plane.

"No," said Ora, "focus, but let go."

Zach stood there breathing heavily.

"But don't do it towards a person," said Ora, "don't want to hurt them."

Zach turned towards a wall without the tv. Just standing there, breathing. Standing, breathing, doing nothing else. At least his eyes are open. We stood there for minutes doing nothing. Just waiting for Zach to do something. Me and Ora sat down waiting.

"Does it usually take this long?" I asked Ora.

But Zach shushed me, was it not right for me to do that? Ora shook her head no, probably to avoid getting shushed. We laughed, but after a minute we got bored because of the waiting.

After another minute he inhaled deeply, before exhaling for like five seconds. He started walking towards the wall, very slowly. Very-very slowly, he got an arm's distance away slowly moving his arm towards it. Oh! Why does he have to be so slow about it?

His arm was several inches before it. His hand touched the wall, only touched. Didn't go through or anything like that. He punched it a few times putting three holes inside it.

"Why!" He screamed.

He stomped his foot and threw his arm all the way through the wall. He didn't take it off, he just punched.

"Why won't you work!" he weeped.

He fell on his knees, holding himself up with his hands. Pounding the ground in anger.

"If i can't do this," shouted Zach, "then what else can I not do!"

He stood up and stomped one of the holo projectors, breaking it.

"I can't do anything!" he screamed.

He covered his eyes with his hands. Leaning up against the broken wall. All of a sudden he punched the glass wall, cracking it. If a fly were to land on it it would shatter. He rubbed his knuckle, bleeding from all the wood and glass inside it. He wiped off some of it before storming out of the room.

I peeked through the door watching the nurse pull the wood and glass out. After that she wrapped up his hand to stop the bleeding. Soon after Zach got into the elevator and left.

"So," I said, "I guess it's just the two of us!"

She looked at me like this had never happened before. Like this was very unusual.

"I hope you don't act like that," said Ora.

I lifted my arms up as if I didn't know. I think I might get a little mad, though I won't act out like that. I don't know how people could present themselves in public like that.

"I guess we'll see," I said in response.

"Okay, your turn," said Ora.

I've been dreading this all day. I don't want to go into the astral plane. I want to learn more about the dangers and excitement about it.

I stepped up to the middle of the room. Oh, why do I have to do this? I didn't know what she was gonna teach me, I didn't want this. I thought it was like war tactics. Not going into a whole other dimension. Why couldn't she have explained it just a little more. Otherwise I wouldn't be in this situation. I don't want to do this.

I can't just say no to her either, she's expecting me to

go through with this. I didn't have a problem yesterday, why would I have a problem with it today?
"You okay?" asked Ora.
So I responded, "I'm a little nervous."

I took a deep breath, closing my eyes. Imagining everything that could go wrong. What if I focus on myself and my clothes fall off. What if I focus on the ground and die. So-so many things can happen to me if I don't do it right. What if something doesn't happen? What if I'm not able to go into the astral plane. Maybe only a select few people can do it. If so, how do you know who can or can't? Well I guess you just have to try.

I exhaled, all my worries going away. Or so I thought! Everything just came rushing at me. Bam! Bam! Bam! All my worries became a thousand times worse. Usually breathing helps people with stress. But it doesn't happen to me. Everything just comes back to me worse than ever before. Well, I'll just put that in my notes. Don't breathe to get rid of stress, don't do that.

At that point I realised I was panting. So I walked to the drink machine and got water. Chugging the whole thing in half a minute. I wiped my mouth off, making it dry. I threw it on the ground, walking back up to the middle of the room. I breathed in and out one last time. I clenched my fist closing my eyes. Instantly opened them again and looked at the wall. Focusing on it, letting go. I relaxed, opening my fist, several black flashes happened. I looked over at Ora with a nervous look. But she just shook her head no.

I shook with each black flash, each only lasting about a second. I tensely looked at the wall, each flash getting longer. Two seconds, three seconds, four seconds, five seconds. I-I think I'm doing it! Though not for long, I'm doing it! I noticed this orb thing, so I touched it. *Boom!*

I flew into the wall seeing flashes of the future. A temple exploding, a monstrous knight wielding an ax. I tried standing up but more future flashes occurred. A death of a friend and one of a secret enemy. I sat down with my hand on my forehead. Ora came up to me putting her hand on my shoulder.

"You Okay?" asked Ora.

I responded, "Yes, I'll try again."

I started thinking about that song again.

The airs just fine
In the evening
But the pain's not leaving
So I joined the army
But that wasn't very long
'Cause I got gunned down
But now, I'll finally be free
'Cause I'll finally be with you again.

God, this song is becoming my life. Though I'm not going to die from being gunned down. I'm going to die from being spit out of another plane of existence. Man, I wonder how painful that will be. Guess I'm going to find out soon. I decided not to touch the orb. I could have been spit out because of orb. Or it's that my body can't be in it for very long. So I guess I need to find out.

"Just do what you did before," I heard Ora say from behind me, "just don't do the one thing you did."

Yeah that seems very helpful, do what you need to do but not. That's the greatest advice ever, such-such a good mentor. I can't believe I have to listen to her. I don't know, I'm just going to relax. Play a little bit of that song in my head.

When the wind blows
Deep at night
Sitting by the fire
Warmness on my feet
Before the wind dies down
But at least I still
Have you besides me

That first part is always so calming. Before everything got up and went to crap. Just relaxing by a fire. A little bit of wind on a deep autumn day. Man, I wish I was there now. I've never experienced autumn before. Though it's starting to turn autumn on this planet. So I can't wait to see what it's like.

"Hey-hey Von!" said Ora, "you okay?"

So I turned around and said, "yeah-yeah I'm fine."

Apparently I wandered a little towards the wall. So I walked towards the middle of the room again. I was getting kinda tired so I rubbed my eyes. I scratched my head before clutching my stomach. It probably hurts from landing on all of those boards.

"Okay let's try again," I said.

I stood in the middle room breathing heavily. All the injuries I've gotten are starting to build up. My foot, my arm, my chest and stomach. Though I'm feeling it alot more in my back and head. But I just got that so it's going to sting a little more than the rest. I surveyed the room to see anything else

I could fly into. The whole room was destroyed. At least we don't have a concept of currency. Otherwise we'd have to pay for all of this. How would that be fair? This is why I'm happy not to be a part of the Zepher Empire.

I got my footing, looking at the glass wall before me. I breathed in one more time. My hands losend to a natural state. All the bad thoughts in my mind left, drifting away. I looked at the wall with extreme focus and determination. I watched the hail stop at the same time my thoughts did. I had a feeling this was it. Everything around me started getting dimmer, with a white outline. Just like my first dream of Martha. I looked down and saw the orb. I got a little scared so I closed my eyes, flinching. When I opened them again I was out of it. I took another deep breath knowing that I could do it. I just need to not touch the orb. I couldn't stop thinking of the orb so I decided to try and stop. I started to think of more happy things to drown out the orb. The first thing I thought of was puppies.

Then I started feeling bad, I haven't seen a puppy in person before. I've only seen pictures of them. Too bad they didn't bring any puppies with them when they left the earth. They all died in the explosion. So I started thinking of other things to drown the puppies out. Wow, that sounded kinda wrong. I thought of that flower field, with all those pretty flowers. Then I started thinking of Elaine, with her smile and curly hair. But I started thinking of my wife. If I went out with Elaine it'd basically be cheating on her. I would never say yes to Elaine, I just can't. I have a wife, no I had one.
"Okay, happy thoughts," I said, " happy thoughts."

I relaxed, staring at the wall. Putting my arm through is my only goal. I've managed to get in the astral plane before. But only briefly, I do believe I can do this. Nothing in my mind besides the wall.

Everything around me started darkening. While a bright white outline surrounding everything. Looking outside the bright purple sky turning black. The two native stars glow extremely bright. All other stars not visible appear. I-I'm doing it! Though it's been flashing in and out a lot. I'm in it but only three seconds at a time.

Beep! I heard from behind me, out of nowhere. It scared me so much, I popped out of the astral plane. I turned around and watched the television flare to life.

"Hello," said president Seaburg in a very bad tone, "I have some terrible news to share with you."

"What?" asked Ora.

Seaburg responded, "We've already contacted Zach about this, but all the others are now war criminals."

"Why?" I asked.

"They blew up an ancient temple," said Seaburg, "so we're sending you guys and Zach on a search party."

"I can't believe they did that," said Ora, covering her eyes.

Seaburg made a motion for us to get out, so we left. We took the elevator to a floor several levels below the surface. We entered a room where Zach was sitting there waiting for us.

"Show him how to do this," said Ora.

Zach responded, "fine, time to show the noobie what to do."

Zach laid out all of our armor pieces on the ground. There were a lot of tiny pieces. Probably to make it easier to move around. Nothing like the gatekeeper armor. Everything was one piece, the chest plate, thigh guard, shin guard. Bicep, and forearm guard. Underneath it was just clothes. Underneath the base armor of this one is like a woven

metal. It's both super flexible and extremely durable.
He started putting his leg into the base armor onesie saying, "First you slip this on."

So I took off my jacket and put my legs into the leg thing. Then putting my arms in the cold sleeves. I wish my shirt sleeves were longer.

"Zip me up," said Zach whilst turning around.

So I zipped Zach's armor while he zipped Ora's. I turned around so Zach could zip mine up. After that Zach picked up the chest armor. Mine and Zach's armor were the same but not Ora's. I looked at the wall and saw the four classes of upper chest plates.

The plasma shotgun armor was thick and square. Probably because you're supposed to be right next to the enemies. All the other armor parts were thick and square like the chest plate. The complete opposite was the plasma sniper set. Which was a lot thinner and really pointed. The plasma derringer and plasma rifle sets were the same. Except for the weapon holsters on it.

They were like the plasma shotgun set except a lot smaller. Parts of the armor had a pointy design like the chestplate and shoulder pads. But to a lesser extent of the plasma sniper set. Last was the captain set. Which had even less armor than the plasma rifle and derringer set. The spikes were a lot more rounded out. There are design holes in the armor design and it was a lot more fancy. It was all gold with little bits of white. It also had a dark black cape with a soft bright red inside.

"You put the chest plate on like this," said Zach.

There's little latches on the side that you open so you're able to lift up both sides of the armor. Then you slip your head in and let the chest plate drop before clamping it back. This armor is extremely strong and super easy to put on. The thigh and bicep armor are the same to put on. The sides also have clamps that you open and have it basically split in two. Except for the hinge that's keeping it together. Then you put one side in the arm and clamp it on. The forearm and shin guards just slip on easily. Last is the boots, gloves, helmet and guns.

“Okay, let's finish up,” said Zach.

First you put on boots, just like regular boots. The helmet just fits over. You then buckle it and lower the visor. After that you just slip on the fingerless gloves. You grab your bag and put it over the shoulder. After that you snap on all the pieces of armor that both protect you and are used for mobility. Then you put your gun into the holster.

“Can you guys help me put on my cape?” asked Ora.

So we snapped the cape onto the shoulder pads. I got one look at Ora and she looked regal. After that she picked up her helmet and put it on. I noticed his base armor was a gun metal color rather than our silver. Also his visor color is a light blue while ours is an orange.

“Usually there's a padding layer,” said Ora, “but not on this mission because it’s just a find and arrest.”

It makes sense to me. We're not going to war, so we won’t need that extra layer of protection. I heard that on these missions most of the time a gun isn’t even fired. On our way out Ora and Zach got their own plasma swords. I didn’t get one though it makes a lot of sense why. Don’t want me to catch fire for no reason on this mission.

We walked out and started making our way. Taking the exact same route they took. Off in the distance we heard loud noises from trees falling. When I first met them I never would have guessed they were vandalizers. I can't believe they'd just go and do this.

We got to the woods and kept walking until we got to the river. Then we started going downstream following the river. Eventually we made it to a bridge that was missing most of its planks. I knew it wasn't the one I destroyed because there's more than two planks standing. We walked a little ways down and found sticks stuck in the ground on either side. We walked across the river because the water only went halfway up the shins.

"Look!" said Zach, "there's a bunch of broken up land and mud on here."

"There's a little bit of blood too," I pointed out on a tree.

"Look at the ruins," said Ora.

I looked over and saw the remains of what used to be a temple. The pillars are only half of what they used to be. That's not an exaggeration, the pillars are literally in half. All the walls were caved in besides one and a half of them. There was rubble everywhere.

"What have they gotten themselves into?" I asked.

Part: 4

The sorrow of death and duel to the cliff

We all stood there staring at Mortem, him staring back. There's a heavily dense forest area on my left side. We could book it there, making it to the other side. I just hope it’s more forest. I looked back at all the others and tilted my head towards the dense forest. They all nodded their heads in agreement. I looked down at my plasma sword, slowly opening a secret compartment to the detonation switch. I pressed it in, quickly throwing it towards Mortem knowing it has a two second countdown. We all ran into the forest hearing the loud explosion from behind us.

We ran up the steep hill making sure to get in front of the trees in case the ax comes flying at us. Though I don’t think the trees will do much. Making it to the top I looked down, seeing the flower field. I-I found it again, that means it’s there. The necklace is still there, my fathers necklace is still there. I knew if I found it everything would be okay. It’s a strange piece of metal, bent and malformed. With a little leather strap that goes around the neck. I rushed down the hill, the others reluctant but following after me. I went to the tree and dug up a little box under it. I slowly lifted up the lid and there was nothing. S-someone stole it, I can tell because the foam insert is gone.

Zoom! I heard from behind me, so I looked up and watched the ax chop down the tree. I jumped out of the way, dropping the box. Syless slid across some heavy mud. Raith ran over and helped Syless up. I looked up and saw Dray ignite his plasma sword. Seth ignited two plasma knives one normally and one spinning it, holding onto it by pushing against his hand.

Seth stepped back and Dray swung at Mortem, hitting Mortem’s arm. Mortem swung the ax at Dray's head, Dray ducking out of the way. He took his plasma sword out as Mortem swung the other way. From there Dray brought up his sword stabbing Mortem in the head, He then kicked Mortem taking his plasma sword out. I swung at Mortem but Seth blocked it, crossing his plasma knives. Did Seth think I was going to his side? I'm not a traitor like he is.

“You can’t kill him, we need to run,” said Seth.

I broke the lock, swiping at his stomach. Though I only got a bit of armor. He swung his right arm causing the tip of the blade to cut my face. It started bleeding heavily so I kicked him in his knee. Then I punched him square in the nose causing him to fall back. After that I looked back at Dray to see how he was doing. Mortem swung his ax at him, he ducked out of the way. He then stabbed at Mortem’s stomach but the blade bounced right off. Mortem swung his ax again so Dray tried blocking it with his plasma sword. The plasma sword broke so he stepped back to let it regenerate.

Seth charged at me so I hit his left plasma knife, causing it to fall. He then tried getting my head but I blocked it bringing my sword up. He couldn’t slide it off and stab me because of the curve in the blade. *Beep beep boop!* I heard a loud noise from behind me. Me, Seth and Dray looked in that direction, seeing Syless trying to contact the others. *Buzz!* I heard from behind me, then I watched a one foot beam strike Seth in his right shoulder.

I noticed in the corner of my eye that Dray looked over at us. So I put my full attention on them then, *Bam!* The ax crashed into Dray’s side, causing him to shift in that direction. He dropped his plasma sword, blood spilling from his mouth.

“No!” I screamed.

I looked back at Seth and another beam landed in his

stomach causing him to fall forward. Seth looked up clutching his stomach when a final beam hit him in the center of his chest. Causing him to fall over dead, dead as a doorknob.

“Ora, Ora!” I heard Syless scream from behind me, “we-we need backup at-at the flower field now!”

I looked back over at Dray and the ax went through the top of his head. The blood spraying across my face and all across the field.

“No,” I said quietly.

Mortem then twisted the ax slightly causing his head to explode. The blood getting everywhere. Then three of Raiths beams hit Mortem, in the shoulder, chest, and forehead. Only putting mere dents in his armor. Syless’s beam hit Mortem too. Only yellowing the armor, so I shot at him with my plasma rifle but it only bounced off.

I ran at Mortem, jumping in the air when he swung his ax at my legs. While in the air I stabbed out his right eye with the plasma sword. When I landed the sword came out, causing his orange blood to spray out. He stepped back covering his eye from the pain. The bright neon orange blood rushed out all over his armor.

I noticed Dray’s plasma blade near his cold limp body. So I picked it up, igniting it, running back towards Mortem I jumped kicking off of his armor. When I landed five feet away I watched him stumble backwards. I swung my two blades on the ground, the flowers flying off burning. Flames coming from the ground.

Mortem made his ground as the flowers hit him. The flowers barely did anything to him, kinda useless. Mortem then stepped towards me swinging his ax. Though I managed to get out of the way before the ax hit me. One of my plasma swords went into the ground, causing all the flowers around to catch fire.

The fire started to burn my hand, so I jumped out of the way. I landed on my stomach in the flowers. Realising my mistake I looked up and saw the flowers catch fire. So I rolled over getting to my feet.

“Come on, we need to go,” said Syless, “they’re on their way come on.”

I walked over as the flower field lit up. There was a big line of fire between me and Mortem. The fire spread strong and quickly. It was intoxicating, I couldn’t breathe. Coughing, gasping for air. He threw his ax at me but I got out of the way. I stepped away as he stepped closer into the fire. The flames engulfed him.

He looked like the devil, horns and everything. Though his horns curve down while the devils up. His armor glowed a deep orange from the fire. I watched as the fire spread, stepping back inch by inch. But Mortem was just standing there.

The smoke was getting so strong, I had to leave immediately. I ran towards Syless and Raith, escaping from Mortem going into the forest. After a while we stopped halfway up a mountain. There was lots of smoke in the distance. It’s gonna get to the forest soon.

We sat up against the tree seeing what gear we had left. Three plasma swords, a plasma derringer, rifle and sniper. We stuck to our standard weapons and each of us got a plasma sword. We had no healing supplies and minimum food and water. Not to mention extremely damaged armor. Syless’s is basically made out of weeds that he tied bits of armor to.

“Five to three,” said Raith, “just like that.”

Syless covered his eyes and started crying. Dray, his best friend in the whole world, died. I can't believe we lost Dray. But we have to move on. I'm going to defeat the N.G.C's and Mortem, for Dray. I can't wait to give it my all.
"We need to make it to the cliff," I said.

I looked at the top of the mountain and I saw something. It was a temple, just like the one the N.G.C's blew up. Except it's intact, even more intact than the one before it blew up.
"Look!" I said pointing at the temple.

Syless and Raith looked up and saw it. So we all decided to go there. Maybe there's a weapon in it like the ax. We started hiking our way up the mountain. All the little needles from the trees disappear. But so are the trees, so we're losing our cover but we're going to get something we need.
"Who's gonna get the weapon?" I asked.
Raith responded, "You are, captain."

We made it to the top of the mountain where the temple was located. It's a little slanted because it sits on the tip of the mountain. So all the weight pushed it down a little. Though there's lots of beams holding it up so it's not going to fall. Syless was the shortest so he stepped on our hands lifting him up so he could get in. Next was me so I stepped on Raith's hand. I proceeded to grab onto Syless's hand lifting myself up. I put my legs on the edge, the stone underneath broke off a little.

But I managed to make my way up. Me and Syless grabbed onto Raith's hands pulling him up. He used the beams as leverage to help him up. We went to walk in the temple, but it was full of webs. Looking in I saw these gold things shining at us.

“Those must be the weapons,” I said while pointing at them.

Raith put his hand in there and started wiping away the webs.

“Oh,” he said while pulling away his arm.

He kept trying to tug it back but he could only go a few inches.

“Something got my arm!” He said, “something got my arm!”

He then flew into the temple without a warning. We heard a loud crash a few seconds later. I tried peering through to see what flung him in. But the webs filled up really fast.

“Spiders!” I said.

I looked over at Syless and watched a web stick to his chest and pull him in. Gods, I hate spiders. A web grabbed onto my legs and pulled, making me fall over. I lifted my arms up as I was being dragged. Mainly to stop it but I just ended up collecting more webs.

I was in the spider's den, and the spider was huge. It was eleven feet tall and twenty feet wide. It took up the whole back part of the temple. The spider started slowly reeling me in, so I ignited my plasma sword cutting the web attached to my leg. I stood up, the spider hissing at me. I swung at it missing, getting my arm stuck in a web hanging from the ceiling.

The spider swung a stinger into my stomach. I fell over with my mouth foaming and eyes watering. I saw Syless and Raith inside the web, awake. I also saw a bunch of skeletons inside the web and a bunch of weapons too. There was a bow and arrow and a pickaxe. All like Mortems armor. Eventually I was trapped in webs myself.

“Fire,” I said to Syless, “fire”

Syless moved around a little bit. Loosening his posture, he put his head against the wall and started moving his shoulders. I tried moving but I couldn't. The poison from the stinger was starting to overcome me. A dim orange light appeared behind Syless, he managed to light a match. The spiders stepped back, appearing scared of the light.

Bam! I heard something hit the temple, Mortem knows we're in here! He's hitting the beams holding up the temple. We're going to slide down the mountain. *Bam! Bam! Bam!* The spider started moving to the otherside hissing.

The right side shifted down, causing everything else to shift. *Bam! Bam!* The temple started sliding. Bam! The ax went through the wall and the temple kept sliding. The temple started sliding fast and Mortem went through the wall knocking him over as the temple was sliding. The whole temple was crumbling.

The only thing I could see left of Mortem was the ax. Then the temple hit a tree on my side. A brick ended up smacking me in the face. The rest of the wall crumbled off. Hitting the tree also caused the spider to fly into the ax. Its blood went everywhere.

Klink! We heard and the temple went up into the air. I went up crashing into the wall, causing my left arm to get free. While outside of the temple I saw Mortem laying a while away. He looked almost dead, even his ax was ten feet away from him. After that I crashed back through the wall ripping the webs attached to me even more. I even crashed through the floor and landed on the muddy ground. But the rest of the floor dragged me all the way to the bottom. I got up at the bottom of the mountain. I still had lots of webs on me and my stomach was bleeding because the stinger was cut in it. My armor was destroyed now, I can't imagine how Raith and Syless are doing.

I saw one of the boots sticking out near the spider's corpse. I walked up to it and saw Raith stuck to a wall trying to get up. I ripped open the webs and got him up. He seemed to be in better condition than I was. Though I guess he was attached to the wall this whole time and the wall just broke off as the temple was sliding.

I started getting a headache but I brushed it off. We walked up a little more and saw Syless sitting there. I grabbed onto his hand and lifted him up. We started walking down the mountain and I ended up fainting.

I woke up leaning up against a tree, Syless giving me the final thing of water. I looked down at my stomach seeing a piece of my cloak from my bag. I gave Syless the rest of my ripped poncho because I didn't need it. He really likes ponchos and he lost his a while back.

Raith came back with a bunch of berries and we ate them down. Raith aso gave me a few different berries that are supposed to cure my poison. I don't think we can stop Mortem now. Though he looked pretty damaged too.

"Look what I found," said Syless.

It was Mortems shoulder pad but slightly mangled up. We-we can use this as a weapon against Mortem.

"We need to get something to extend this," I said, "To make it a spear."

Raith said, "While berry picking I found a old blacksmith shop"

"We should use that, let's go there," said Syless.

We got up and started walking there. The forest down here had a lot less needles. Though those kinds of trees aren't around this part. After a few minutes we made it to the

black smith shop next to a little pond. I found a little sign, so I removed the fulliage seeing the name. Orfield black smith.
“Isn’t that your last name?” asked Syless.
I responded, “yes”

We walked to the shop seeing the web filled trees behind it. On the front there's an anvil and a sword holder. There's also shelves and walls that weapons are attached to. Everything coated in a layer of dust., except for a few footsteps leading to the stone path we took to get here. Though they were really small, couldn’t have been my fathers.

We opened the creaky door, revealing a room with more weapons. Noone could have raided the place, everything is intact and layered in dust. None of these weapons could stop Mortem though.
“What are you doing here,” we heard in a young woman's voice from behind us.

It was all scratchy and quiet, she must have needed a drink. I turned around seeing a five’ four girl with brown hair. No more than eighteen years old. She was wearing a light pink button up shirt and light grey pants. Also with a bright white apron.
“We need to get in the bunker,” said the woman, “they’re coming.”

She went to a floor board slightly up and lifted it open. She then climbed down the ladder underneath the board. So me, Syless and Raith followed.
“Close the hatch,” she said, “there's smaller ones that can fit through that.”

So Raith closed the hatch and we looked around. It was a grey concrete room, twenty by twenty feet. There was a small kitchen on one side and an old man in a bed on the other side. On the other side of the old man was a door that led to the bathroom. There was also a door attached to the kitchen that led to a herb garden.

“That’s mister Orfield,” said the woman while pointing at the old man.

I slowly walked towards my father, watching him cough up blood.

“What is your name?” asked Raith.

“Joy,” responded the woman, “I’m mister Orfield’s daughter.”

“Who’s the mother!” I said instantaneously.

Joy responded, “I don’t know, he told me he ran off with her.”

At least it rules away the possibility of she being my sister. Though she's still my half sister. After we defeat Mortem I’ll bring her to our building to stay. I walked back to my father sitting at his bedside.

“Hello son,” I heard my father say, “I’m sorry.”

His heart rate started slowing down.

“I love you,” he said, “you know what to do.”

I responded in a confused tone “what?”

“The knight,” he said, “Joy spotted him and alerted me of his presence.”

“What does that have to do with this?” I asked.

“The book,” he said, “it has everything you need to know to stop him.”

“But we don’t have a weapon to stop him,” I said, “only his shoulder pad.”

He said, “good.”

Maybe he’s going to make it for me.

“This book teaches you how to blacksmith,” he said while giving me a book, “bring the stuff down so I can watch.”

“What stuff down?”I asked.

He responded “you know, you know.”

So me, Syless, and Raith climbed up the ladder. We grabbed five weapons and handed them down to Joy. We then pried the anvil from its stone slab and dragged it into the room. Raith was the strongest so he stayed in the room. Me and Syless climbed down to set the anvil. Raith pushing it down the hole, I and Syless holding it up with our hands.

The anvil was too heavy for us so we jumped out of the way. Syless pushed away Joy because she was in the anvil's path. The anvil slammed on the ground creating sparks and cracking the ground. Raith then climbed down, closing the hatch behind them. We then moved the anvil to its upright position and pushed it away from the ladder.

“Couldn't we just have done this stuff up there,” said Syless while pointing up.

“No,” said my father, “the spiders would wake and kill you. They are sensitive to light and sound.”

Joy walked over and turned on the fireplace.

“Put the weapons in there,” said my father, “it doesn't matter what it’s made of. That stuff can cut through anything, even itself.”

So we put the five weapons in the furnace and turned it up. It was going to take a minute so Syless asked Joy to see the herb garden. Syless is the youngest of the group, only nineteen years old. He got out of training only a year ago. He was the replacement for Wess. So I don’t know why we needed Von and Seth to join us. Usually we only have six on our team.

“Get the staff mold and welding torch out of the closet,” said my father while coughing up a bit of blood.

Raith put the mold and the welding torch on the anvil. So we sat down waiting for the weapons to finish melting.

After a few minutes Syless and Joy came out of the herb garden and sat down next to each other. We waited around for half an hour doing nothing.

“They’re done now,” said my father, “grab the tongs and take it out.”

I grabbed the long metal tongs grabbing the hot tray that caught the melted metal. I slowly poured the melted metal into the mold, only spilling a little bit on my boot. It only took fifteen minutes for it to cool. So we took it out of the mold and broke off the stray metal bits.

Then I sanded the parts where the stray metal was. I swung it around for a few minutes to get a good feel of it. I’m so glad that I took a staff course while in school. Now I just have to add the spear head. I put the shoulder pad face down on the anvil and placed the staff where Mortems shoulder went. Raith had to sit there and make sure the staff was straight. So I grabbed the welding torch, getting ready to weld something together for the first time.

I moved down my left thumb, igniting the welding torch. Immediately turning it off and covering my eyes. I heard my dad laugh in the background as I got my vision back. He then threw some goggles at me. Who knew flames were that bright.

“You’re supposed to wear those,” he said in a laughing tone.

So I put on the goggles, igniting the welding torch once more. With a hammer in my other hand. For a few minutes I moved the flame around in the same place until it started to melt. I hit the side of the shoulder pad with the hammer. Moving it a little towards the staff with every hit.

I did it until the shoulder pads edge got close to the staff. But by then I just had to let it cool. While it was cooling

I hit down the edge until it touched the staff. Once it cooled I torched the edge of the shoulder pad attached to the staff. I did it until it melted, so after that I waited for it to cool. Once it was cool I did it to the other side as well. Doing the exact same thing, torching it while hitting it in. Then I welded the rest of the shoulder pad to the staff. Then I waited awhile until it dried. I then put the shoulder pad to the grinder, giving it a prominent point.

I then swung it around a bit until I almost dropped it. So I grabbed some leather and gave it a grip. There was a lot more leather so we decided to give ourselves better bandages. But Joy brought out some gauze and wraps for us. So we ended up replacing all our wraps with fresh ones. That was probably a good idea because they were all tattered and bloody. Soon we heard a loud crash, and we could only infer it was Mortem.

"Stay down here Joy," said my father.

My father gave Raith a bow before the three of us climbed up the ladder and into the room. We noticed Mortem through a window so we got our weapons ready. Watching Mortem, until he disappeared. All of a sudden the head of Mortem's ax went through the wall. Mortem then took his ax out, removing half the wall with it. We ran out the door and to the forest. Looking behind me I watched as the rest of the black smith shop got destroyed by Mortem.

"Run!" Raith yelled at us while loading his bow.

He shot it at Mortem causing the arrow to go up in flames before hitting Mortem in the shoulder. Mortems whole upper right side went up in flames. He swung his ax around causing some of the fire to go out. Mortem grabbed onto the arrow ripping it out, his orange blood pouring out all over his armor.

The fire went out revealing a melted mess. His mask was all disfigured and droopy. His horn was a hollow dark brown with kindles of fire. The spike on his right shoulder pad drooped down touching his shoulder. The right side of his chestplate was all melted and disfigured. His right arm armor was all melted and holey.

Mortem lifted up the golden arrow, snapping it with his thumb. Raith shot a few more arrows at Mortem. But Mortem blocked them all with his ax. But one hit Mortem in the shin causing him to lean forward. He threw his ax at Raith but he managed to step out of the way before it hit him.

Mortem walked a few steps over grabbing onto his ax and pulled it out of the ground. Raith shot him a few more times, causing Mortem to catch fire. When the fire cleared Mortem was on his knees, blood oozing from the cracks in his armor. The rest of his silver armor yellowed, his deep crimson eye peering at us. Loudly breathing in a menacing tone, a few coughs here and there.

“We need to leave Bly,” said Raith.

We ran into the woods, the webs getting thicker and deeper the more we went in. We had our guns at the ready in case a spider jumps out of nowhere. Such terror in a maladic situation. How can one bear to stand at the thought of what has happened. But thy shall continue on, for it is my mission to murder Mortem and crush the N.G.C’s.

Using thy spear I shall vanquish him, slitting his throat. Chopping off his head, and arm limb by limb. Until he’s nothing more than a pile of body parts. I’ll take his armor as my own, and put his skull on a shelf like a trophy. Under that armor he’s nothing but a fleshy monster.

We heard rustling in the distance, so we fired our guns in that direction. Raith’s plasma bolt zoomed bringing down webs and branches putting a hole in a tree. My plasma bolts scattered hitting the general area of where we heard the rustling. Syless's plasma bolt hit something causing it to bleed. The spider leaped at us missing a leg. The spider knocked down Raith and started gnawing at him. Syless had the reaction to fire again, hitting the spider straight in the head. We then kicked the spider carcass off of Raith helping him up.

"Why does it have to be spiders?" I whined.

Syless responded, "once we get through this forest we'll reach the cliff."

"Couldn't we have gone along the forest?" asked Raith.

"No," I responded, "we'd be in the open, so Mortem could easily get us.

"Instead of walking further in, we should just keep going the way we would need to go."

"That's a plan," I said, "we're gonna avoid more spiders doing that."

So we walked through the forest, a peep not said by anyone. All frantically making our way, trying to make the least amount of noise as possible. After a few minutes we made it to a bunch of thick webs. So I grabbed my spear and started cutting away the webs. We advanced forward getting rid of all the webs we can. Though some of the webs still managed to get stuck to us.

While walking through the heavy mess of webs a web stuck to my spear and started pulling. So I and Syless shot at the giant spider. The giant spider proceeded to fall to the ground, clearing away a few webs. Though the spider was in our way so I stuck my spear under it and moved it over into the webs. We continued walking through the forest.

I was happy because we are halfway through the forest. We're away from Mortem's grasp but once we meet up with the others we'll go back and murder him. After the webs cleared up there was a tiny thin tree in the way. So I chopped it down with my spear.

It crashed to the ground revealing another spider. It was a lot smaller than the other spiders. It ended up jumping at me, but I impaled its head with my spear. So I flung it into the distance, clearing up more webs for us.

"Jumping spiders," I said in realisation.

Syless asked, "Do you think there's a queen?"

"I hope not," responded Raith.

We continued walking, collecting more webs on our legs and shoulders. While walking through I realised how out of shape we are. Syless doesn't even have a helmet and his armor is being held together by weeds. I have holes and cracks in my armor, with bandages holding it together. Raith's doing a lot better, though he has a big gaping hole in his hand. I'm surprised he can even hold his gun.

All of a sudden I saw Raith fall over at the corner of my eye. I turned towards him and watched him get dragged across the ground. He was gripping his neck because the web was around it. So I shot deep in the woods trying to kill the spider.

Syless grabbed my spear and started stabbing at the ground. Before he could hit the ground again a web grabbed the spear. He held onto his spear with all his might as he was being pulled up. After a minute he let go crashing to the ground. A web grabbed my arm and I pointed my gun towards the spider.

But another web grabbed my gun and pulled it away.

Syless grabbed onto my arm and we tried pulling it back. But Syless fell face first knocking me over on my side. Syless started sliding away, web attached to his foot. He got dragged away clawing at the ground. Before I knew it he disappeared into nothingness.

I tugged with my arm one last time as a web hit my chest. I started getting dragged along the muddy floor myself. I kept moving around trying to escape, but I got tangled within the two webs. I looked at the spiders and watched them reel me in. I proceeded to tug one more time and hit my head against a tree.

I woke up hanging from a giant tree. I looked around, noticing a lot hanging too. There were a few more giant trees, I looked down and saw a giant web attached to each of the trees. In the center was a giant spider, four times larger than all the others. I also noticed that Syless and Raith were hanging upside down themselves.

I started getting a really bad headache from the blood rushing to my head. I also noticed the weapons hanging as well. I started thinking of a plan, my plasma sword was still attached to my belt. Luckily my arm was tied up there. I feeled around for the button and ignited it. I felt the blade burn up against me. I also felt my webs loosen so I swung my right arm. My body twisted, breaking out of the webs. My arm attached to the webs is the only thing keeping me from death. I swung around uncontrollably. My only option is to swing to the giant branches next to me.

So I started swinging until I had enough momentum. At the moment I did I cut the webs my arm was attached to and flew. I hit against the tree, dropping my plasma sword. I cut my cheek against the bark of the tree before landing on the thick branch below me. Some of the leaves attached to it fell below. I got worried because I realised I dropped my plasma sword. I looked around and saw it got caught in a web, I was so relieved.

I noticed five spiders climbing towards me along the webs that attach the trees. The only thing I have left to fend them is the plasma sword. I reached towards it but my arms were too small. The spiders inched closer every second. I moved slightly off the branch causing it to bend. The spiders came closer and closer, but the closer I got to the plasma sword the more the branch bent.

By the time I was close enough the spiders were here. So I grabbed onto the plasma sword and tried prying it from the webs. But I realised if I ignited it, it could cut through the branch. So I ignited it, swinging it behind me into another spider and cutting it in half.

The other four spiders stood before me ready. So I grabbed onto the branch and slid off of it. From the momentum I swung up, stabbing another spider. My feet stuck to the tree and pulled out my plasma sword. The spider fell to his death, never to be seen again. I cut off a few legs on another spider and cut off the bark that my feet were attached to.

It caused me to swing to the other side, cutting off the side of one face. I ended up swinging back, kicking the spider with a few missing legs in the face. Thankfully it broke the bark in half, causing my legs to be free. While swinging to the other side I cut off the branch the other spider was attached to.

But the spider grabbed onto my legs, sinking its teeth into my right leg. The immense pain caused me to let go of the branch, making I and the spider plunge to our doom.

But thankfully I ended up smacking into a dead person hanging up in a web. Finally not falling I stabbed the spider until it died.

I twisted around to see the other side and saw the spear a jump distance away. So I pried myself away from the sticky web. Though it ripped the web a lot causing the dead body to be free. I almost fell because the web wasn't attached to any of us. But I grabbed onto the web and bent my knees. I jumped towards the spear, the dead body behind me plunging into the abyss. I grabbed onto the spear with all my might, making sure not to let go. Otherwise I'd fall into the abyss. Unfortunately I was swinging uncontrollably so I got spotted by more spiders. Climbing up the tree and to the web the spear was attached to. So I continued swinging, hoping to stick the spear into the tree right next to me. So I took the leap, with the web snapping.

My spear drove into a spider and the tree behind it. A few hundred feet away hangs Syless. But he's too far away to jump. The only thing I need to do is climb up the rest of the tree. So I grabbed onto the thick web attached to the tree and hung the spear on my shoulder with its strap.

I continued climbing up the tree, worried that it would tear off. I got up about twenty feet when a spider came at me. So I ignited my plasma sword and with a simple swipe, I sliced off the left side of the body. Though the right side didn't fall into the abyss because it was trapped in webs. I continued climbing up with my body hugging the tree. I didn't want to fall so I made sure the webs got stuck to me. Though it also removed the web from the tree bark. I climbed until I got high enough so that the leaves poked me. I looked down towards Syless and realised how high I was.

I was dizzy with concern, one wrong move and I'm done for, we're all done for. Though I saw a hanging web rope a jump distance away. So I ripped away from the webs still stuck to the tree and leaped. I grabbed onto the web rope and swung. Falling down towards Syless because it snapped from my weight.

I stuck to his web rope and I fell back. The webs on me got stuck to the web holding up Syless. So I was hanging upside down, with a bit of my strength I pulled myself up grabbing on. I ripped my webs from the ones holding him up and started climbing down. Inching down very carefully, I didn't want it to snap because I'm in charge of two lives right now. Once I got down to him I ripped open the webs he was entrapped in. He almost fell, but I grabbed onto his poncho to stop him. That woke him up and he started swinging his arms. So I pulled him up, close to where he was.

"Grab on!" I yelled at him.

He grabbed onto the web and we decided to make our ways to the weapons. We would have gotten Raith but he was pretty far away. Once Syless got ready we climbed up the web to the top of the tree. We looked out in the distance, overlooking the rest of the forest.

I noticed that even though these trees are way bigger than all the others, they all stop at the same height. So I pieced together that these trees grew in a canyon. I gave Syless the plasma sword so he had something to defend himself with. Once we got to the edge of the top of the tree we jumped to the next. Syless managed to grab onto a branch, but I didn't. I didn't fall because I stuck my spear into the tree. Though I was at the end of my spear so it started bending from my weight. So I inched to the tree, starting to climb up. But a spider tackled me, knocking me down to a branch below. The spider pinned me down, so that I could only move my left arm. The spider hissed, getting ready to bite.

I started smacking it with my left hand as I noticed Syless going flying from the tree. Syless fell smacking against the tree sticking, dropping the plasma sword. So I reached out, grabbing it. I then stabbed the spider, pushing it down to the abyss. I watched a spider climbing down to Syless, getting ready to strike. So I threw my spear at it.

It just missed the spider and almost hit Syless. The spider looked at me before advancing towards Syless. So I grabbed onto the webs and started trekking my way up. Once I got far enough up I stabbed the spider through the head using the plasma sword. I grabbed onto the spear for leverage and cut the web attached to Syless's foot. But to my mistake, he started falling.

Freaking out I immediately threw my body against the tree. My plasma sword going deep into the tree. I looked down at Syless hanging below me. I grabbed onto the web attached to the foot and swung him down to the branch below.

I took out the plasma sword while grabbing onto the spear. So I put the plasma sword on my belt and jumped down to the branch below. Syless was still knocked out so I put him up against the tree and wrapped him in webs so he wouldn't go anywhere.

I looked towards the weapons and realised the weapons were close. So I put my spear on my shoulder, getting ready to jump towards Raith's gun. The branch snapped behind me as I leaped towards the plasma sniper. My form was immaculate.

I grabbed onto it swinging, I hit it in a way that made it fire. The twelve inch plasma beam zoomed by my leg and down below. As I got to the end of my swing I watched as the beam hit the queen. What a terrible thing that I have done. While swinging back to the tree I grabbed onto the plasma rifle.

So as I got back to the tree I cut the web attached to the plasma sniper with the plasma rifle. Thankfully I landed on the rest of the branch below. I put both the plasma guns around my shoulders and smacked Syless awake.

“What?” Said Syless.

So I responded, “We have to go, now!”

I helped Syless up and we jumped to the next tree. Looking up I noticed Raith was only a tree away. But a tree away was also hundreds of spiders and the one behind us, spiders. Below us spiders, above us spiders. The spiders were surrounding us. I gave Syless the plasma rifle so I could grab my spear. We moved across the webs connecting the trees before jumping, sticking my spear into a spider. Syless landed on a spider crushing it. Then he fired his plasma rifle, killing a few more spiders.

I sweeped with my spear, sending the spiders flying. While they were flying Syless shot them down. I stuck my spear in a spider and jumped to another branch. Syless shot a few while jumping over too.

“Hold them off!” I screamed, “I'll get Raith.”

I stuck a spear in the tree for Syless to hold onto and I prepared to jump. I leaped, and a spider tackled me. As I started falling to my death I lifted my arms up. My only chance of survival was to grab onto Raith. In that moment my whole life flashed before my eyes.

A happy childhood, until my father left when I was

very young. My mother turning to drugs sent me to military school. I went through years and years of training. Just to find out my mom died and the truth of why she put me in that god awful place. Right after getting out of military school I joined a squad, just to see my best friend die right before my eyes. Just to be replaced by an arrogant self-centered jackass that I hated the whole time at military school. All of those jokes, and mocks about our system. I always thought he was a traitor, until I truly met him. Where I liked him enough to save his life. But a few years later my hatred of him got replaced by a kid who didn't know anything and his friend, an actual traitor.

If it wasn't for him I wouldn't be in this situation. Mortem wouldn't have been resurrected, Dray wouldn't be dead and I wouldn't be falling to my death. It's all his fault and I'm glad I squashed him like a bug. All of a sudden I hit a tree, snapping me awake from the trance.

The spider tried saving itself so it webbed to a tree. But-but it's still stuck to me, then I had an epiphany. The spider couldn't detach because of the webs stuck to my back. So I kicked off the tree causing us to swing. When coming back I dodged the tree to get more momentum. Once I had enough momentum I cut off half the spider, sending me flying towards Raith. I hit him and hugged his legs so I wouldn't fall. Then I climbed up him so I wouldn't fall. Once I got up to Raith I started ripping the webs from his body. Pulling the webs around his head down as if it was a hood. Once he was loose I started swinging us to jump to the tree. But first I'll have to wake him up. Though I was hoping the swinging would. At last he woke up, hurling out food. He almost fell off the webs but I grabbed onto him. I pulled him up and said, "we need to jump now."

So we leaped to the tree, landing on the sturdy branch. I handed Raith the final plasma sword and I took my spear from the tree. We were destroying the spiders but too many of us were on the branch, so it was starting to snap. So as a last ditch effort Syless lit the tree ablaze. The fire spread rapidly because of all the webs attached.

We all jumped down, catching ourselves on the webs of the tree. But we needed to get down fast because the fire was heading towards us. So we kept letting go to get further and further down the tree. But once we got close enough we jumped to the web attached to all the trees. We looked up and watched the fire spread rapidly to the other trees.

So much so that ash was raining down on top of us. We made our ground and looked towards the spider queen. She was furious that her nest was being burned down. She hissed, I was sure we were going to die. *Zoom!* I heard at my side and I watched Raith's plasma bolt strike the queen.

It put a deep hole in the queen and Syless shot her as well. But it only put little burns on the queen. So I grabbed my spear getting ready to strike. But the fire has spread down to us, all around us. It was closing in on us, the fumes taking over my lungs.

Syless and Raith kept shooting at her, doing barely nothing. *Snap!* I heard and realised that the web we were standing on was snapping. So I grabbed onto the web and told the others to do the same. *Snap! Snap! Snap!* We started to fall, the deep chasm below swallowing us. Now I know this is the end of me.

I woke up at the bottom of the canyon, still alive. I was in a very small section of it. On one side of me was the wall, the other was a very burned section of a tree. Probably part of one of the giant trees. I looked around and found my spear. It's good just in case anything is still alive.

So I got on top of the hot tree and looked out over the rest of the canyon. It wasn't as big as I thought it was. Though it was still pretty large. The queen was slumped on the ground, still alive-barely. The corpses of dead spiders were everywhere. Within the vast amount of dead bodys I noticed Syless.

He was lying there, sprawled across the ground. He didn't look alive so I ran over to him as fast as I could. I rolled him over and looked at his bloody nose. He was still alive, but barely. I got down on my knees and started giving him CPR. I gave him a few slaps during which shocked him awake.

Syless grabbed onto my arm, breathing heavily. So I helped him up and we looked towards the queen. We just decided to put her out of her misery so I took my spear and drove it through her head. I took it out and realised something. Raith was missing.

"Raith!" I yelled, "where are you?"

We sweep around, lifting up tons of dead spiders to see if he was under any. After looking under them all we didn't find him. So the only other place he could be was under the queen. So I stuck my spear under the queen. Rolling it over, at last he wasn't under there.

"There's a crack in the canyon there," said Syless, "maybe he got up and made his way there."

So we walked by the mass of spiders and squeezed into the gap. After a while it loosened up and we got to the end of it. Raith wasn't there either. So we climbed up and made our way to the ground. With no sign of Raith up here we decided to go along the canyon just in case. So we made our trek, looking down to see if there is any higher bit he fell on top of.

After a few minutes we walked along the whole edge, nothing. So we slid back down into the canyon, on the side I started on. We looked around the basic area and I didn't see him anywhere. We looked into one of the crevasses but he wasn't in there either. We peered into the other one and he wasn't there either.

The only other place he could be was the tree. So I grabbed my spear and started chipping away at the tree. It was easier than it would have been because it was charred. But I still didn't do enough damage. So I ignited Syless's plasma sword and put it most of the way through the tree. I didn't want to go all the way through in case he was actually under it.

Then I just used my spear to cut through the rest. Though what I saw he wasn't under that area. So I slammed my spear in the tree and started pushing it. But I wasn't strong enough to push it. So Syless grabbed onto my spear and we started pushing it as hard as we could.

At last it moved slightly and we started to see Raith's gun under the tree. So while I was holding it in place Syless jumped forward and grabbed onto his gun. He pulled it out and Raith wasn't there. The tree just rolled over and it fully revealed he wasn't there. So I took out the spear and looked towards the other part of the tree.

I grabbed onto the plasma sword and cut the tree in half by the top. After that I stook the spear into the bottom of half the tree and flipped it over. Raith wasn't under there either. So we climbed back up and noticed another tree knocked over. It wasn't as big and thick so it was easier to move. So we decided to push that over, maybe Raith is underneath that one.

So we got down and started pushing with our bare hands. After a minute it rolled over revealing a bunch of leaves. Disappointed, I got on my knees and they consumed me. In an instant I fell through them into a small human sized hole. I fell through, hitting several jagged rocks before landing into a small puddle at the bottom.

Half soaked in mud I looked up towards a humanoid figure. It was a skeleton, so I screamed and jumped back. Arms of another figure went around me, so I jumped to the other side looking back. Finally, I found Raith. I was so relieved he was still alive. I crawled through the muddy water, shaking him in excitement.

"Hi," responded Raith.

From above I heard Syless say, "you okay?"

"Yes," I responded, "we'll be up soon!"

I got on Raith's hands, lifting myself up high enough to climb up. I got seventy-five percent up when I grabbed onto Syless's arm and lowered down my spear. Raith grabbed on and climbed up it before he got to the climbable rocks. So I got to the ground, keeping my spear down as a lifeline for Raith. But he managed to get to the ground just fine. From there we got to a tree and started peeling away our dirty webs. After that we got a good count of our supplies. The only weapons we have are the plasma sniper and rifle. The plasma sword and the spear. We have no food or medical supplies and very little water. I have very little hope for what's to come.

After getting together we started making our way towards the cliff. Walking through the extremely bare and damaged woods. On our way we found a patch of raspn'weeds so we sat down near them and started devouring them. We were so hungry we couldn't stop eating. We hadn't had food in hours. At least I haven't, I can't speak for the others.

"This is so good!" said Syless.

Raith responded, "such a good first meal for the day!"

First meal? I know we didn't have breakfast when we left but still. You'd think they would have had something today. Though now that I think about it we left yesterday and I've been with them the whole day. So I guess I haven't eaten at all today either. Though these days have been blending together. Maybe I have hit my head or something? I wonder what my medical evaluation is gonna be like.

From behind us we heard a loud crashing noise. So we all turned around, seeing Mortem. He was only a little bit more damaged with lots of webs covering him. Drooping off his horn and wrapped all across his armor. He was angry, gripping onto his ax. Looking at us with intensity he threw it at us. We rolled out of the way and watched as it cut a few trees down.

Raith shot at Mortem a few times. Only putting mere dents in his armor. The ax flew back into Mortem's hand as Syless swung his plasma sword at him. Striking him in his right forearm doing nothing. From there he stepped back so his plasma sword could regenerate. I charged at him, dodging a swing from his ax before stabbing him in the abdomen. He swung his ax again but I shifted so he only cut off the end of the spear.

I then proceeded to jump out of the way, ripping the spear right out. He clutched onto his heavily bleeding stomach, stumbling back. Raith and Syless shot at Mortem.

Causing him to step back with each hit from Raith's plasma sniper. Syless's bolts just kept bouncing off of him. So I jumped back towards him, dodging another blow from his ax. I went to strike him in the side and missed. So he kicked my spear out of my hand and he swung his ax again, I barely got out of the way. I then slammed into his stomach, causing him to fall back on the other side of a sideways tree. Realising where we were I rolled the tree a few feet towards me as Mortem was getting up. He then swung at me again, missing as I jumped onto my feet.

Mortem fully up, started walking towards me. Lifting up his ax getting ready to strike. Once he was gonna take his final step he fell, smacking his head against the ground. I watched as the rest of him fell into the hole, smacking his back against the stone wall. His ax got caught on the ground, I was a little nervous but the stone broke sending it down into the pit. I then pushed the tree over the hole, hopefully ensuring he'd get stuck there for a while.

I looked back towards Raith and Syless, smiling while putting my thumb up. I walked back towards them, grabbing my spear along the way. I put it around my shoulder and got back up to the others. So we started making our way back to the cliff. Keeping our guards up, in case something else happens.

While getting closer and closer to the cliff the trees got bushier. With the forest getting thicker I got nervous with what could be lurking in the forest. Any spider still alive, any giant snake. A god awoken from the burning trees. Anything could be in here, anything could be watching us. Anything could be following us, anything could be waiting to strike.

From there the terrifying malady of thoughts struck

me left and right. How can one be fine walking through this forest? The mystical terrifying tone looms across the woods. The dance between what could be a threat and what could not. I don't know how I'm so very nervous now. Especially when I was not before.

Snap! I heard from around, terrified I turned around throwing my spear with all my might at it. My spear had struck a Dawnyte. A deer-like animal that only appears at day. So pulled my spear out, turning around seeing the cliff a little while away.

Zoom! I heard from behind, so I turned around and ducked out of the way. Mortem had finally caught up to us. Syless ran up and started shooting at Mortem. Mortem responded with a swing of the ax. Luckily Syless dodged it, but Mortem managed to get the plasma rifle. So Syless pressed the button on the plasma sword, throwing it at Mortem.

The plasma sword exploded in front of Mortem. While Mortem stepped back distraught Syless ran a little out of the woods opening his computer. So Raith started shooting at Mortem. I charged towards Mortem, dodging a hit from the ax. I crashed into his stomach falling to the ground. Mortem stepped back in pain so I shoved my spear into his calf. I pulled out the spear and kept stabbing it. Ripping into it until I saw the bone.

Mortem fell back in pain with each and every stab. He got on one knee, swinging his ax back in response. The ax struck my spear, cutting off the head, leaving the head in his leg. Realising the spear failing I smacked the rest of the staff against his head, breaking it in half. So I kicked Mortem down onto his back.

I ran out of the woods with Raith, so close to the cliff. Just need to go down the hill and through the final section of the woods. Mortem came running out of the woods in intense rage. We all got out of his way while he swung the ax. I shoved Mortem out of fear, pushing him down the hill. The butt of Mortem's ax crashed into my stomach. I crouched down as I watched Mortem tumble down.

Hitting against rocks and smashing his face into the ground. A god, just falling down a hill, in such a way that would have killed a human a hundred times over. Hitting everything, putting dents into armor and gashes into skin. Before finally at the bottom slamming into the tree. He went sideways into it, the tree crashing into his stomach. With so much force it broke in half.

"You okay?" Syless asked me while I was on my knees.

I looked down at my stomach, I thought it was bleeding heavily when the spider hit me with the stinger? This was on a whole other level. Blood gushing out, I was getting light headed. My mouth was dry, I felt almost as if I would faint. Raith took off his poncho, wrapping it around my stomach. Tying it tightly to stop the bleeding.

We heard branches breaking behind us as the sun was setting. Raith and Syless put my arms around their shoulders and started bringing me down the hill. Running past Mortem who was on his knees, leaning against a tree. The light shined brightly against my eyes. Leaving spots in my vision. The trees started deforming and twisting, everything around me turning evil.

"He's dying!" I heard a god scream in the distance, "he's dying! We need to do something!"

My blood gushing out all over the evil forest. But one of the trees snatched me, trying to eat me alive. But the two gods freed me from it, trying to save me. Giving me cpr, putting glowing sticks into my arms to save me. Everything around me, twisting and contorting. Everything staring at me, the deep orange sky. The grey trees with bright crimson leaves, the same color as blood.

The dead black grass, everything around me catching fire and heating me up. Oh the pain of the fire engulfing me. Tis but a sad end to my lonely life. Never able to complete my goal of destroying the N.G.C and killing Mortem. But thy can watch on as my friends and colleagues do so. Watching from the bright white heavenly above.

But thy Satan slowly walked towards me. I tried speaking out, but not a word transpired. Pointed with all my might to the ghostly guel. His hellish eyes peering at us. Atlast the gods noticed, dragging me away from the devil. They were saving me, saving my life. Stopping me from going to the burning pit of hell.

But thou shall not pass through those gates. Thy will escape from his grip and live on another day. Satan got knocked back by one of the gods while the other kept dragging me to the Outer World. Away from the darkness and to the deep orange light. Keeping me away from hell where I surely belong because of all the things I've done.

But I've done thy things purely for good. To benefit the cause of the U.G.C. But alas it comes at the cost of joining the white heavenly above. But it's something I'm ok with, for the right of everyone. To stop the Zepher's and everything that opposes the U.G.C. Keeping peace is a good exchange to go to hell.

Satan swung his sickle at the god before falling cold stone dead. The god came running towards us, helping the other god drag me to thy Outer World. But Satan was not done with us yet, the devil cannot and will not be killed. But there is still hope, still hope to escape the devil's grasp of my life.

Hope has finally prevailed, three more gods appeared behind Satan. The devil got up and hissed at the five gods. All readying their weapons, except one who got on his knees to help me. The five of them were all staring at each other, waiting to see who will make their first move. The gods or the devil, but one thing was certain. There was going to be a blood shed.

Part: 5

The clues from few hours past

We stepped into the temple ruins, everything completely destroyed. A bright golden casket at the end, jewels all around the ground. There were like a dozen bodies laying all over the ground. In two different kinds of clothes, there were the ones in robes and the ones in black painted armor. There were a lot more guys in robes than armor. Looking closer at the armor it was just like the U.G.C's. They looked almost as if they just spray painted it black. I grabbed a stone off the ground and started scraping it against the shoulder pad. The paint is just peeling off in clumps.

“What's that?” asked Ora.

She started walking towards the casket like she just noticed it. She grabbed onto something in the wall and started pulling. She started kicking at the wall, a little bit of dust spilling off. She turned around and grabbed onto a gun one of the robed ones was holding onto. She got up close to the wall and pressed the trigger. A weird purple beam came out of it and as soon as it touched the wall it exploded.

Ora flew back a foot or two, landing on her back. A parade of rocks and dust fell from the sky. A big dust cloud was all around the area. We all watched the cloud waiting to see what was in the wall. Ora stepped into the cloud disappearing. But the cloud subsided soon after, revealing Ora grabbing onto something.

She pulled and the wall broke fast allowing her to step back. She was so surprised with how easy it got out that she dropped it. It made a distinct clinking sound, it was unlike any metal I've heard. Ora leaned down, picking it up from the ground. She turned around and lifted it up towards the sky. Revealing a giant sword, the blade was seven feet long. It had a nice chrome blade and a golden hilt. It had two red stones embedded in the guard of the hilt. It also had a weird scripture along the blade, it was unlike anything I had ever seen.

"Well that's cool," I said, "But what in the world do you think came out of that casket?"

I walked up to the casket peering inside. It was a red velvet color, in the shape of the person inside. It was seven feet long, it was kind of hard to see its figure because it fit a cape inside. But you could tell it was wearing some kind of helmet. Room for distinct horns that curved down. I looked towards the top of the casket, flipping it over. The red velvet wasn't cut, I guess I really didn't need to say that.

It's hard to think about what could have come out of this, whatever it was was terrifying. It had to have been a god, it could have been Malus because his sword was near it. But Malus was trapped in Mortem's ax, considering the casket had cutouts for horns it must be Mortem.

"We need to hurry," I said, "they're probably dead already."

I turned around and noticed something holding up a part of the wall. So I walked over, grabbing onto the wall with both hands. I lifted it up just enough to slide the thing out with my foot. I picked it up and it was a ratted old book. The cover is all torn up and unreadable. I turned the pages to the bookmarked one, there was a hole in the page and where there wasn't a hole the words were worn out.

I don't know what it says, something about dogs or something. On one page was a drawing of a knight, with horns that curled down. Probably the thing that came out of the casket. There were more spikes on it than I expected. Looking at it I wondered what else was in the book. Turning the page was another character, also referred to as a dog. Dog, wait a minute, it's backwards.

"It's backwards!" I blurted out.

These words were all faded, but I could barely make out this page. It was about a god named Malus who wielded a sword. My suspicions were confirmed, the swords are the same. It says something about a brother named Mortem who wielded an ax. Which must be referring to the guy that was in the coffin. I was right. They seem to have brought destruction and chaos wherever they went. But they got stopped by gods wielding a hammer and a shield.

The next page goes over the god with a hammer. The hammer god's name is Fauna. It states that her temple is in some part of land I've never seen on a map before. It's nothing like anywhere I have ever seen before. It wasn't very flat and there were three volcanoes. It says she guards some kind of Heart Stone. But other than that I couldn't read much more. It was the most intact page so far, but it's still pretty worn out.

"That has a map of the restricted zone," said Zach.

I responded, "restricted zone?"

"Yeah," he said, "it's a part of the land separated from everything. We're supposed to stay out because it's considered dangerous. I think it's all of the volcanos. Actually we're heading close to there. The cliff is right across from the restricted zone."

"Interesting," I responded.

I turned the page to the shield god. His name is Chronimoir and he guards the Cuchillo. So the Cuchillo escaped its prison somehow. I touched the shield of the god who guarded it. That must have been how I contracted it. Remnants of it stuck to the shield managed to enter my

bloodstream. Probably from the burns I received just after touching the shield. So Seth was right in that hospital, when we meet up I'll tell him. But he touched the shield as well. "What's the side effects of having Cuchillo in your bloodstream?" I asked.
Ora responded, "increased anger, mood swings, rash decisions, why?"
"No reasons," I responded.

I wonder what kind of trouble Seth's been getting into. Though he hasn't cut or injured himself so it hasn't entered his blood stream. Though he could have gotten a small one I didn't notice. I didn't get any of the side effects, though it wasn't in my system long. It could have reached his brain by now. But he could be fine, knowing him, he is.

I turned the page again, and it talked about a duo of gods. The sisters are called Mas and Menos. They both wield bows, Mas uses an ice bow and Menos uses a fire bow. Instead of having to use arrows you just have to pull back the string and an arrow materializes. There's even an option to shoot three at once. But the bows seem to have an energy meter, so you can only use it a certain number of times.

They seemed to have the most amount of information available. Though the page definitely isn't as worn out as the others. I turned the page again, revealing the final god. His name was Vigor, he was a mining god. He has a pickaxe and a mining helmet. It's said that he mined tunnels all through Valor's underground.

He even dug the chambers for the heart stone and the Cuchillo. Clearly the Cuchillo's chamber wasn't built as well. Though it could have been human interference that opened it. The temple did get exploded by a human search party that came to Valor. That could have been why the Cuchillo came to Earth, another party came down searching for them and the Cuchillo got on their ship.

They're considered heroes but that's why we're here now. That's why so many species died, because we still wanted to live. We the U.G.C are the bad guys. Maybe the N.G.C's are right, them and the Zepher's are the good guys. I can't believe it, everything I thought and stood for has been a lie. All my life I believed we were good, I need to make a change. Though first I need to follow orders, once we defeat the N.G.C's I need to convince the others. Then we can strike and defeat the U.G.C, but we can't do it by ourselves. Maybe with the help of the-the Zepher's, no I'm getting ahead of myself. We will get there when we get there. I just need to build up their trust, but I shall never speak of this. I might need to do this by myself. So I placed the book in my satchel for future reference. Let's move on and find the others, that's my first and only objective. Who knows if I'm even right.

Ora put the sword on her shoulder for support and we left the scene. The way we needed to go was probably the one with a few trees knocked over. There were at least three knocked over and a few more along the way. After a while there were footprints going diagonally. Probably when it started to hail.

"This goes into the direction of the cliff," said Zach.

So we kept going until we found a circle of trees fallen over. The trees themselves were sprawled all over the place and there were prints going around the stumps in two directions. In the middle was a knee and leg print plus a foot print. Not too far away was a gash where the ax must have gone into. They seemed to have tried to stop Mortem with trees, though clearly that strategy failed.

It looks like they lost their ground because the prints started going diagonal to the left. Walking by there was another tree knocked down, a person seemed to get stuck under it. Looking closer it must have been one of the guys. The poncho included with the pouch was stuck under it. Looking closer there were tiny bits of armor stuck in the ground too. I hope my leather jacket doesn't get all ripped up during this. Though I probably shouldn't have put it on over my armor.

"They must be in bad shape," said Ora, looking at everything.

I looked in the distance and asked, "what's that?"

I ran over to it and picked up a piece of a horn. It must be part of Mortem's helmet, it was a lot bigger than I expected. Though it definitely wasn't the whole thing. I stuffed that in my pocket along with the book. We kept walking in that direction finding another place where someone fell over. Going a little ways up the hill was a small crevice of land going down. At the bottom was a little stream of water before leading to another hill. So we continued down before landing in the muddy water. Going up the stream until it stopped. From there going up the hill was a bunch of muddy prints and slides.

"Wow, look at that," I said.

Back on Rozz it was a rainy day. I was probably only twelve years old, and didn't have any friends. So I always went out exploring, trying to find secret treasure. One day I snuck into the goldmine, ducking into little creavousis. Going through I found this green gem sticking out of the wall. I tried pulling it out but couldn't.

So I took my pocket knife out of my pocket. Sticking it into the wall, trying to pry it out. I figured I had to take out the screwdriver from the other side. Stabbing it into the wall, trying to get it loose. But I was only able to chip away at the rocks. But after a while I was able to get it loose enough. So I stuck the knife in between the wall and the stone. Pulling it out as hard as I could. The metal bending from the pressure.

Once it popped out my blade snapped, so I wasn't able to grab onto it. The stone fell, falling in between the floor, landing in a net filled with gold. So I snuck out of the creavous, peering out at the large cavern. It was giant. Everything was gold, no wonder why it's so inexpensive. I grabbed on a rope near me, looking down at the net being lowered into a cart and dragged away.

So I grabbed onto the rope, sliding down to the tracks below. Staying low so nobody spots me, once I got close enough I jumped onto the cart. I started ravaging through all the gold to find it. A lot of gold has gone on since then and alot more on the way. A piece of gold even hit me in the head. But after a few minutes I found it.

"Hey!" I heard in the distance, "what are you doing."

I was spotted, so I grabbed onto the gem and jumped onto the tracks. The guy was coming after me so I pushed the cart towards him. It smacked into him, causing it to fall over. So I started running, them chasing after me closely behind. They were coming from both sides so I jumped off the tracks, grabbing onto a rope. Swinging back and forth until I grabbed onto the wall. Slowly inching my way to the boards, eventually I got there, So I ran out the mine's door, running up the mountain it was in.

The rain crashed down upon me, causing the ground under me to slip with each step. All the mud sliding down the mountain, the guards behind me tripping. Once I got to the top I realised I could jump into the mud, hiding from the guards. So I went face first into the mud, going down faster than I expected. The rain was just too strong, the dirt on the mountain was all being stripped off.

I kept going through the mud until I crashed into the mud at the bottom of the mountain. Intrapped in mud I looked up at the guards, starting to fall down the mountain themselves. I managed to get up from the dense mud, so I started running. But there was a problem, I was getting close to the fence and going past that was illegal. But there was a nice forest on the other side of that and they hadn't identified me. I was sure I could just hide in there until they were gone.

So I went to jump the fence, grabbing onto the top to get leverage. Unfortunately I got shocked, at least I got on the other side of the fence. Looking through the fence the guards were getting closer. So I got up half paralyzed, dragging my foot across the ground. Getting in deep enough until I found a nice sturdy tree. Grabbing onto a branch with my working hand I slowly got up to the branch. I got up two more to be safe, but the guards still found me.

All of them got their guns jammed by the mud. So they started hitting the trees with their clubs. They started climbing up themselves, so I continued climbing as well. But they were able to climb up faster than I was because of my paralysis. Out of nowhere I heard a buzzing noise above me.

So I slowly climbed up trying not to disturb them, until I got above. Then grabbing onto a branch I jumped down to the branch the hives were on. It cracked and the bees started coming up towards me. Not wanting to get stung I jumped two more times, causing it to fall. A few of the first bees that came up and stung me in my neck, wrist, and cheek. But thankfully the branch fell on them, so the bees kept stinging them and causing them to fall off.

Starting to lose my paralysis I started to go around the tree to the other side. Jumping tree to tree, trying to escape them. Once I got to the final tree I jumped to the other side of the fence. Looking back and seeing the guards chasing after me. So I darted back towards the mountain, going around the bottom. But it proved difficult because of all the mud.

So eventually I decided to run up the mountain. Pushing the rocks down the mountain to hit the guards. Until I got to the top, revealing the extremely damaged town. After that there was no more rain, everything drying up, all the trees dying. I'm so glad to get off that dying planet. We didn't know it then but the atmosphere was collapsing. That was the last storm we ever had before everything dried up.

It pulled the dirt from the mountains. Once I got the call to come here I was ecstatic. Finally able to leave the dying planet and not die with everyone else. There were no ships on that planet, but that is just a U.G.C rule. They didn't care about my planet, that's why they let it die. The only people they helped were people from the first two towns. Didn't care about the others because what they did was more important. Reaching into my pocket I take out the green gem. In all these years I've done research on it. They called it an Emphite. It's a very special kind of emerald that is said to have magical properties. I placed it back in my leather jacket for safekeeping. Looking up the hill I was back to reality. The mud on the hill really reminded me of my past. But nevertheless I have to stop thinking about that and get my head in the game.

My main goal is to find my friends and save them from Mortem's grasp. I put my foot in the mud and started walking up the hill. Each squish reminds me of my past. The time when I once was a troublemaker, before I became a gate guard to stop people like my past self. It was either that or a gold miner and I hated being in that mine ever since that day. We finished going up the hill until we made it to a rock. It was ginormous and had a few prints on it. On the other side was a little hole that could fit a few people inside it. There was also a bunch of dirt piled up, they must have hid here to hide from Mortem. The prints could be from Mortem, which would explain why they were a little big.

There were prints going down so we started following them. After a while there were a bunch of raspberries on weeds. Quite a bit of them were picked off, they must have had a snack here. There was also a little campfire with a bunch of uncooked rabbit meat around it. Whoever made it must not have been a good cook.

"I'm confused," said Ora, "we are going the opposite way of the cliff."

"Maybe they decided to go around the forest," said Zach.

I responded, "we should keep going to see where they go."

So we continued going, finding a knocked over tree with a crushed beehive. A crushed beehive, there was also another knocked over tree. It looks like someone was under it. Continuing we made it back to the temple. But a tree near us had a bunch of blood on it, I wonder what could have happened here. We decided to turn back, eventually making it to the rock.

We found some other footprints that we hadn't seen

before. Eventually we made it to the mountains, going through what they call an underpass. But it is really just a tunnel going through the mountain. After going through it we walked a little up to the square top of the tunnel. There was another campfire and this time it was bigger.

There was a little spot where they sat down and a few trees a little uphill were knocked over. Looking down at the field was a bunch of burn spots. Probably from them shooting at Mortem. We continued walking through the woods uphill until we found another tree knocked down. It was a lot bigger and it had a gash in it itself. So we continued walking through the woods until it was broken up from the field. So we kept going until we saw some dead N.G.C's.

Most of them seemed to have died from plasma knives. Must have been from Seth, he was the best knife thrower on Rozz. That's how he got the food for him and his family. He was asked to go to two but he decided to stay back at five. Though a few of them did look like they died in different ways. The guards were cold, so we were definitely far behind them. Maybe a day behind, they all could be dead by now.

We continued walking to the forest on the other side. It looked like an explosion had happened in this area. All of their prints were in the ground, so we know we didn't miss any dead bodys. From there their prints seemed to have gone up the hill. Something about this area was oddly familiar, almost as if I had been here before. Or at least close, we continued looking up the hill. Looking out at the burned flower field. This is why the area seemed so familiar. All the beautiful pink and white flowers were burned to ash. The old tree was just a shell of what it was. All that beauty is gone, just like that. I can't believe this happened. Though I guess this was the only way for them to protect themselves. It must have slowed Mortem down quite a bit.

"Looks like Syless's handiwork," said Zach.

Only confirming my suspicion that they did this to protect themselves. Walking down we noticed something lying there. We walked up to it and it was a slightly burned corps of someone. On closer examination it was Dray. I can't believe Mortem killed Dray. I rubbed my eyes in disbelief, I can't believe this happened. I didn't know much about him, but with him being anti war he definitely hated dying like this.

"Dray," said Ora, "not you."

Ora started to tear up, her best friend just died. She took off his left shoulder pad, throwing it towards the chunks of Dray's head. She then removed Dray's shoulder pad and attached it to herself. She then proceeded to rip off the dog tag and placed it around her neck. Ora then pounded the ground with his fist, picking up ash with her hand. Loosening her hand, allowing ash to pour out.

I wonder how the others are dealing with this? I hope they're doing okay. They must not have time to mourn because of Mortem chasing them. But we will destroy him for killing our friend, we have a god's sword that can kill him. Right now I have to help these guys with this.

"The others are dead," said Zach, "the others are dead!"

"No-no-no don't like that, they're probably still alive," I responded.

Zach yelled! "Probably! Probably!"

That's not good, I didn't mean it like that. I need to be more careful with my wording. I can't just stand here and say nothing while he's yelling at me. Like I-I didn't do anything, this isn't my fault. Why-why didn't I go with them, if we just went with them this probably wouldn't have happened. We'd be fine, nobody would have died. This is all my fault, I can't believe it.

"Leave him alone," said Ora sternly.

I fell to the ground, sitting on my butt. What have I done, this is all my fault. I put my hand on my forehead, everything getting to me. I had my own friend murdered, I'm going to kill Mortem. I got up and kicked a rock, it skipped on the ground until it hit something metal.

"What was that," I said with worry.

We all rushed to it, revealing a burned shell of armor. Two plasma knives attached to it. Seth's armor, just laying on the ground. What could have happened to him, I hope he's okay. But there was something strange about this armor. This armor shouldn't have burned this black. I picked up a rock from the ground and scraped it against the armor. The paint peels off from the armor.

"Seth's a part of the N.G.C," I said, "he's on their side."

He's had the same worries I've had. He feels the same way I do, he has been thinking the same way. I wonder how long he's thought this way? But why is his armor just laying here? What happened to him? And why are the three plasma burns in his armor. Did he resurrect Mortem? My best friend killed my new friend. Could I have done something to cause this? No, he wouldn't have resurrected Mortem to kill people. He probably figured he would have listened to them. But you can't control the god of death. I'm sure he would have come out and convinced me to join him. I'm just watching as all my friends die around me.

All my friends, die around me

I think I got it, I'm thinking of the final part of the song. What should I do to figure out the rest of it? Oh, I don't know, I should. Maybe I just need to go through the rest of the song. Then and only then I can get there.

When the wind blows

Deep at night

Sitting by the fire

Warmness on my feet

Before the wind dies down

But at least I still

Have you besides me

Just like a normal night of my life.

When the wind blows

Deep at night

The days almost near

The winds gone down

But you're still beside me

Each and every line I hear it come closer to what my life is now. How is this so similar to my life and what's the purpose of it coming back to me? I just need to figure it out.

The winds gone out

The sun is rising

Day's finally here

But before I knew it

You were no longer
Besides me

When everything changed, when my wife died.

The air is steady
In the mid-day
A drop of rain comes down
Sending chills down my spine
The sad thing is that
You're not besides me

The sadness starts to loom over, showing its true strength.

The air stands still
In the afternoon
I went to get my jacket
'Cause the rains pouring down
This rain just shows how i'm feeling
I'm cold and
The sad thing is that
You're not besides me

How the sadness doesn't stop, how it does not relent. It just keeps pouring down.

The airs just fine
In the evening

But the pain's not leaving
So I joined the army
But that wasn't very long
'Cause I got gunned down
But now, I'll finally be free
'Cause I'll finally be with you again

How I gave up, how I decided to leave the dying planet. I will eventually give up, there is no hope.

The air is gone
I watch the sun set
When I thought there was no hope
Watching my friends die all around me
Watching, delaying as much as I could
Before finally leaving
Finally free
Finally reunited

This song has become my life, what is the meaning? There's no hope, what have I done? I-I have no idea what I'm doing with my life. Just in this war to die, doing nothing. This cannot be my life, I do not want any more friends to die. Or at least I'm going to die trying.

"Von," said Ora, "Von!"

"What?" I said finally snapping into focus.

Zach responded, "We need to keep going, we don't know how much time we have left."

So we got up, continuing past the burnt tree. Going through the woods until we stood before a mountain. Slowly making our way up the steep incline. Walking up until we made it to the top. Revealing a destroyed temple sprawled out across the rest of the mountain.

“Oh my god,” said Ora quietly.

Thinking, I dug out the book from my bag to see which temple this is. Going through the pages, the only one with a picture of the temple was Mas and Menos’s. Which is drawn to have a temple at the top of a mountain. Other than that it just appeared to be a regular temple.

So I placed the book in my bag. Then slowly stepped off, going down the mountain. Hand up so I don’t slide because of all of the dirt. Walking past big stones with webs attached. Eventually we started seeing other things, besides the stones. We found a skull that was slightly caved in. A mace lying across the ground, next to a pile of bones.

A spear was stuck into a stone, wrapped in webs. Going down further was a little gold blade sticking out of a stone. The rest of it must be under the stone. Even further was a giant spider laying there. It was huge, probably six feet wide. Huge fangs and a tiny stinger.

Next to it was a bunch of tiny pieces of armor. They were probably inside the temple when it slid down. This must have damaged them even more than they already were. I wonder where this spider came from? It reminds me of The legend of the spider, deep within the golden cavern. What a spooky tail from my childhood.

Legend has it that there is a ginormous spider deep within the gold mine. None other than Vincint Van Vladderhorn discovered it. He was none other than a standard gold miner. He had a tan shirt and pants. Each a little tattered from working all day. Black boots and belt, with a dark brown poncho covering his right shoulder. He also had a dark orange mining helmet, he wielded both a shovel and a pickaxe. Pale white skin and long brown hair. It was said his muscles were as strong as steel.

It was just a normal day in the mine, just a little chillier than usual. Walking down the tracks when out of nowhere he heard a boom. So he rushed down with other miners. Once they got down they found a miner laying there, cold dead. He used dynamite without supervision and didn't tell anybody.

There was a little crack in the wall, you could barely see inside. But Vincint knew something was on the other side. So the whole day he chipped at the wall with his pickaxe, by the end of the day he wasn't even close. So day after day he went back, chipping and chipping at it. Until one day he was able to peer into it. He noticed an extremely blurry and big figure. But it quickly got covered up by something gooey.

When he went home that night, he did some research looking at books. Looking through he found nothing, he even asked a few friends. But nobody could guess what it was. Nobody knew because it wasn't from this planet. Vincint realised the only thing he could do was keep digging until he got to it. So he kept digging at it, but it was taking so long so he got some help. Day after day they kept chipping away. More of this weird gooey stuff came flying out, sticking to the wall. Touching it, it was super sticky. So Vincint cut off a piece and brought it to the lab. After a few days the test results came in. It was unlike anything they had ever seen, it was almost alien.

The doctor told him that it was likely to come from ancient Earth. Something called a spider, he said a few must have gotten onto the ship. He said that the deep depths of the mountain was probably why it survived. As for the sticky stuff, it was called a web.

With this new knowledge Vincint looked at a book. The spider freaked him out, it was unlike anything he had seen before. From there he had a goal. A goal that no one had on that planet before. He was gonna do the unthinkable. He was going to be the first one on Rozz, to kill a spider.

So he headed down, pickaxe in hand. He went to the wall and slammed it in, over and over again. This time chunks came out of the wall. He just kept hitting it, over and over again. Dulling the blade with each and every strike. He was going very hard on that wall.

Until the head of the pickaxe broke, sticking to the wall. So Vincint threw his pickaxe on the ground, grabbing onto his shovel. He kept smashing it into the wall, trying to scrape it off with each strike. The shovel was only for dirt, so it wasn’t able to do much. But it still did something. But not enough, so he went and grabbed a few pickaxes to go at it.

The whole rest of the day he hit the wall as hard as he could. By the end of the day he broke all of his pickaxes. Not worrying because somebody else repairs them at the end of the day. So he kept doing it every single day, still getting nowhere. It seemed almost as if the stone wall wasn’t stone anymore. Probably something alien, maybe the spider brought it with him

So he kept going at it every single day, until one day the pickaxe reached the other side. Vincint quickly pulled out his pickaxe and peered in. He stared at the spider head on when more of this web shot out. Hitting his face and going everywhere. He could barely breathe because it was all over his face. Then the spider pulled hard, making him smack against the wall. Knocked out in an instant.

He woke up the next day with a severe headache. The doctor told him he had a concussion, so he couldn't work for a while. This infuriated Vincint, he was going to be the first one to kill a spider. Now someone is gonna go through the wall and kill it themselves. Vincint could not let this happen. So he snuck out in the middle of the night. His pickaxe and shovel in hand, ready to take on the spider. He snuck through security and ran down to the wall. Clearing the webs before smashing his pickaxe into the wall. It took him all night, but by morning the wall was gone. Him and the spider were staring at each other and Vincint knew it was on.

The spider is dark black, with long hair. It had a weird metal helmet, with tons of electronic green eyes. It seemed as if it was covered in armor. Almost like the weird wall on the other side of the stone. It looked nothing like the spider in the book. It was evolved.

"You dare challenge me!" said the spider.

Vincint readyed his pickaxe, ready to attack the spider. The spider lunged at Vincint, Vincint parrying with his pickaxe. The pickaxe went straight into the spider's leg, it screamed in response. Vincint swung his pickaxe at the spider again. But the spider dodged and parried him by stabbing him in the gut with its stinger.

Vincint fell to the ground bleeding heavily. The poison slowly moving to his brain. As the spider gripped him with his webs and dragged him towards it, he stabbed the spider in its stomach. The blood sprayed out onto his face. He got free and swung the pickaxe at the spider's head. But it bounced off, only putting a mere dent in his helmet.

By now the toxins have reached his brain. Everything started contorting around him, everything becoming twisted and ghostly. Everything became strange, he was becoming insane. Vincint swung his pickaxe again, cutting off a leg of the spider. With more blood spewing out the spider tackled him. Nipping at him with his sharp fangs. By now Vincint couldn't tell the difference between what's real or not.

Vincint kept his pickaxe up to the spider's jaws. Only getting free by kicking the spider in the stomach. Getting up he hit the spider with his pickaxe again, knocking off half of the helmet. The spider leaped at him again, but missed because it's missing a leg. He swung his pickaxe on its abdomen, breaking the pickaxe. So he turned around his pickaxe and kept smashing the flat part into the abdomen. But it didn't do very much, the spider turned around tripping Vincint. So he fell to the ground, dropping his pickaxe. As he was getting up the spider tackled him again. The spider getting ready to strike.

The spider attacked, but Vincint rolled out of the way. He picked up his shovel and smacked the spider in the side of its head. He whacked at it again and again. Losing his mind from the venom. After a while the rest of the spider's helmet fell off. Attacking it with all his might the spider fell into the wall causing everything to shake. Tons of rocks came crashing down onto them. The spider stared at Vincint while he was trying to squirm away from the rock he was trapped under. So the spider started gnawing at his head. But the helmet was in its way. So Vincint stuck his shovel in the rock, attempting to lift it up.

But the shovel snapped, he was trapped. So Vincint started swinging around the rest of the shovel in hope to kill it. Out of nowhere the shovel slipped out of his hand, flying into the wall. Even more rocks started tumbling down, Vincint watched as it crushed the spider. He finally killed the spider. But he was trapped.

Vincint laid there for hours, steadily losing oxygen. But people were digging through the rocks, trying to save him. Vincint grabbed onto the shovel's head and started smacking it against the wall. Trying to help chip away at it himself. But the rocks the spider was under started to move. The spider started squeezing through the rocks.

So he started stabbing it with his shovel's head. The spider's armor must have allowed it to survive. So he went at it with all his might, just so it wouldn't kill him. Surprisingly the rock his leg was under loosened. It was finally free, so he slipped it out and jabbed the spider in the eye. Again and again until it died. His goal has been reached, but his oxygen was depleting.

The miners managed to get him out before it was fully depleted. But by then he had already passed out. So they dragged him out and brought him to the hospital. After a few days he had awoken, most of the venom in his system gone. But to his surprise, nothing. No-one to congratulate him, no rewards, nothing. It was almost as if it didn't happen at all.

The next few days, still nothing. Maybe he didn't actually kill the spider. Or maybe the spider did die by the rocks and they just didn't find it. It could have been a figment of his imagination when it squeezed through. It could have just been from him losing oxygen or maybe from the venom.

The doctor came in and told him about what happened. He said that he was probably hallucinating because of the spider's venom. Which happens more times than you realise, you have no idea how much spiders poison people. He said that if he was left unattended any longer he would have died. So he was very lucky to survive. After a few more days in the hospital he was let loose.

When leaving he finally got the recognition he deserved. He was told that he was going to have a ceremony. Celebrating the fact that he was able to achieve something that no one on this planet had done before. But he still had to wait a few days. He was so excited to see what he got.

After a few long days he finally got his ceremony. He wore a nice suit and got a plaque. So people did actually know he killed a spider. He was so ecstatic, everyone was excited for him. He was the most famous person on Rozz. "Von," I heard Ora say, "Von!"

She snapped me out of my trance. I peered at the giant spider, almost exactly like the one from the story. We decided to get up and keep walking, being careful to avoid the rubble. Eventually making it to the bottom where there was broken up dirt. Almost as if somebody was dragged across the ground. Eventually they made it to another tree with a little bit of blood on it as well.

Must have been from the person being dragged across the ground. There also seemed to be a stone path leading into the woods. They followed it to a broken little shack. It seemed to have been broken down by a giant ax. They must have been hiding in here but Mortem found them. There was a little sign that said it was a blacksmith. I wonder what kind of things it made.

When we came to this planet we definitely had enough technology to make guns. So why would we make medieval weapons? I don't know, maybe just for fun. I wonder where the anvil is though? There was a little hatch in the ground, but it seemed to be locked so we couldn't get inside. It's probably just a small storage space. We decided not to break open incase something inside it is bad. We learned our lesson from last time.

We continued walking and there was a huge burn circle. It had a few broken arrows around, they must have gotten hold of Menos's bow. Other than that there was other stuff too. But what it was, was indecipherable. So we decided to just keep moving on.

"What's that," said Zach pointing at something.

So we walked towards the shiny object, it was hanging off of a tree in the woods. It was Menos's bow, so I picked it up and pulled the string. The arrow materialized out of thin air, then it shot out. The arrow flying before landing on the ground. The ground went up in flames, so we all ran over and stomped on it. Putting out the fire, so Zach took the bow away from me. I'm not good at shooting arrows, so it's best for him to use it.

He gave me his plasma rifle to hold onto so we would have more fire power. We continued into the heavily webbed forest and I finally realised where that spider came from. We followed their tracks and there were a bunch of dead spiders along the way. We kept going until their tracks just stopped. I wonder what could have happened to them. Hopefully they're fine, I guess we gotta keep going and find out.

It seemed almost as if they started getting dragged through the forest. The spiders must have gotten a hold of them. Now I definitely think that they are not okay. So we slowly trekked through the webs, making sure no spider came and jumped us. Though it seems that there weren't any spiders around. Where could they have gone too?

"This is weird," explained Ora, "it seemed almost as if they went somewhere."

Clearly there should be hundreds, if not thousands of spiders in this forest. All we have seen are a few dead ones in the beginning. Something is wrong, I can feel it. We can all feel it, this heavily webbed forest should be bustling with spiders. But nothing here, the ominous atmosphere just taken away. Almost as if something came through here, and took it with it. It must be Mortem, but I don't think it was.

So we kept going through the forest, continuously thinning out. The trees get more ghoulish each step. Almost burnt, there was fire. We kept getting closer and closer as the leaves thinned out. The trees got more crisp and there was a bright light ahead. So we walked towards it, revealing the cleared forest.

"Now this is the work of Syless," said Ora.

Syless burned down an entire section of the forest. I can't believe he did something like this. Hopefully to escape Mortem, he did it with him at the flower field too. Looking back and forth a lot of the forest seemed to have burned down. A huge creavous of land going from left to right was cleared out. You could only put a quarter of the spiders in this forest here.

We seemed to be a little way from halfway. The end closer to us seemed to have a giant thing there. So we had to walk that way. The thing seemed to be a quarter of the creavous. As we got closer and closer it seemed to be a giant hole. As we were getting there, there was this giant log over another hole. So we pushed it over and peered inside.

It was kind of dark so we lit our flashlights and pointed down. There was a muddy, murky water infested with snakes. A human skeleton and a bunch of bones were

floating in it. A large scratch was in the wall, probably from Mortem's ax. They must have tried to trap him in there, but judging by the hole in the wall he obviously managed to escape. Boy I wouldn't want to be inside of there.
"Absolutely disgusting," said Ora.

We continued, until we found a giant hole. So we slid down until we got to the bottom. There was a giant tree, splitting the hole in two. There wasn't much in this section, just a clump of broken armor pieces. Somebody has probably fallen in this hole. There were also two creavousis on this side.

So we peered into the first one, but we couldn't see the other side. So I snuck into it myself. It was very small, so I had trouble going through. But eventually I made it far enough to see the other side. There was just a rat, chewing on a piece of garbage. So eventually getting out I started moving into the other creavous. I didn't need to move as far this time to just see a rotten carcass of a spider.

So getting out, all of us looked at the tree. It seemed to have been cut in half a few times. So we all climbed over the tree and saw the horror on the other side. Hundreds of dead spiders covered the entire floor. It was sickening, I just wanted to get out of there. There was also one ginormous spider there, they called it the queen. A lot of these spiders were burned and disfigured. This was the most amount of spiders I have ever seen. At least we now know why they were missing from the forest. They must have rushed in here when the trees caught fire. Probably to protect the queen, it's what the minions do.
"Man," I said, "Syless can do a lot of damage."
Ora replied, "now you know why they call him the man of flames."

I guess it really makes sense why he's called that now. First the flower field and now the forest. He can really do a lot of damage, I wonder what he could do when it comes to people? It's probably a lot more strategic than lighting a few flowers or webs. He probably sneaks around with a can of gasoline. Splashing it all around his enemies, without them even knowing. Just to light the match and watch them light up in flames.

There was one final creavous in the hole. So we carefully stepped through the sea of carcasses. One slightly alive spider started poking at me. It was only half alive and it was begging to be killed. So I picked up my plasma derringer, slowly pointing at the spider. Covering my eyes as I pulled the trigger. The sound and smell of burning flesh terrified me. I can't believe I just did that.

But it was asking, it was half burned, half crushed. I just wanted to put that poor creature out of its misery. I can't believe I'm just making its murder okay. My foot started to burn a little, until my plasma derringer shut off. So I holstered my plasma derringer. Though my foot still had a burning sensation. So I looked down at the spider and it was still alive. It's still alive!

My foot still feeling like it was burning, I looked down. Since I wasn't looking I ended up shooting myself in my foot. I started getting a headache so I leaned up against the wall. I watched as Zach killed the spider and Ora walked up to me.

"Give me your foot," she said.

So I lifted up my leg the best I could.

"Take your shoe off,' said Ora.

She examined my foot, she was surprised because I managed to get the beam in the right spot. Though the boot doesn't have as much armor. Besides, you're less likely to get shot there because most of the time they're stuck in the mud. Ora took out some bandages and wrapped my foot up. She couldn't clean it because she didn't have the supplies. On this planet only medics can carry medicine on the battlefield. Even though they used medical supplies earlier.

So I put my shoe on and snuck into the creavous. There was only a bunch of moss on the wall. So I got out and we started looking for a way out. We climbed over the tree and started going up the way we came. It was a lot harder than climbing down, but there isn't anything to grip onto. After a while we made it to the top and decided to start going the other way.

Walking towards the other way we started hearing lots of banging. So we got our weapons ready. Ora with her sword, Zach with his bow and me with my plasma derringer. They must have been just ahead of us.

"The cliff is just straight ahead," said Ora.

So we just kept walking towards it, nervous to encounter the god. On the way we spotted more rasp'n weeds. Also with lots missing, they probably snacked on them before encountering Mortem. Though they looked fine, only a thin layer of ash was on them.

"Man," I said, "I'm nervous."

We saw their heads running down the hill. But eventually we couldn't because they got too far down. All of the crashing must have been from Mortem. Pushing him down to damage him, but he's a god. But we have the weapons to kill him. I can't wait until he's dead, he killed my friend. He killed our friend, vengeance will be ours.

The air is gone
I watch the sun set
When I thought there was no hope
Watching my friends die all around me
Watching, delaying as much as I could
Before finally leaving
Finally free
Finally reunited

At least there could be an upside. I need to give it my all, he needs to be defeated. If we don't defeat him everyone on this planet will die. It is our duty to destroy him. This is our one and only chance to defeat him. With each step the song just plays in my head. It really really is becoming my life.

"This sucks," I said.

"Is there anything we can do to give us an advantage?" asked Zach.

"No," said Ora, "I don't trust you guys using the astral plane."

I asked, "why?"

"You've only popped in and out of it," said Ora, "if you try too hard you can get stuck in it."

With that knowledge I knew we were in danger. Without using that Mortem could kill us in one shot. Just like the song, Mortem's going to kill me. Then before I go to heaven I'll watch as everyone else dies around me. Then I'll continue to watch while Mortem kills everyone on this planet. So the song just keeps seeping to my mind.

When the wind blows

Deep at night

Sitting by the fire

Warmness on my feet

Before the wind dies down

But at least I still

Have you besides me

I just can't believe it's actually becoming my life. What's the meaning of this song? Am I just making it up as I go because of something that's going to happen. Or maybe it is real and it's based on my life. But why did my wife sing it in the dream? Maybe the one thing I want to do is leave and be with her.

Maybe there is actually just another meaning to this song and I just have no idea. Maybe there is no meaning and it is just stuck in my subconscious. It's almost as if this song is making me more nervous to fight Mortem. I would be fine without this song in my life. I want it to leave, but it just won't. It's just like some kind of fungus, it's just kind of there and I can't get rid of it.

The air is gone

I watch the sun set

When I thought there was no hope

Watching my friends die all around me

Watching, delaying as much as I could

Before finally leaving

Finally free

Finally reunited

The final stretch of the song reaches my brain as I get to the top of the hill. As we got to the ground we noticed a shiny thing. The sun was setting at the right spot to shine the light into our eyes. As we got further down, who and what it was was racing through my mind. But it became very clear when it started to move.

On a rock we were standing near was a bright orange blood. It definitely wasn't human; we knew it was Mortem's. Out of nowhere a giant ax came flying towards us. We all managed to duck out of the way, only sliding a bit on the rocks. For the first time we saw the giant beast Mortem was.

As Mortem slowly walked the ax flew back into his hand. From there he seemed to slow down, limping a lot. So we got up and I looked at my scuffed jacket, from the rocks. But I immediately shook it out of my mind and we continued further. Once we got to flat ground we saw the other three in the background. Zach fired his arrow at Mortem, striking him in the back of the shoulder. Mortem didn't even flinch as he caught fire. He kept slowly walking towards the others, with a fierce intention to kill. Syless was back trying to contact someone as Bly was on his knees. Raith just stood there with his plasma sword ignited. You could tell they were on their last straws.

Mortem kept slowly walking, his ax scraping against the ground. Ora readied her sword, getting ready to strike. I fired my plasma derringer, but it just bounced off of Mortems armor. That made me extremely worried, how can we beat him. We kept making our way, if we don't stop him now, they're dead. Zach fired another arrow, striking Mortem in the lower back. This time Mortem noticed and looked back at us.

We have entered the gates of no return.

Bridge: 1

The battle of the almighty gods!

Captain's log number infinity, stardate 2693, eighty-five days in. The whole world has changed in front of my own eyes. The trees ghoulish, the grass is snake infected. There's a massive hole behind me and the sun is beating down on my face. I can feel my eyes burn from the rays of the sun. My stomach is in immense pain, I can feel it spread throughout my entire body.

Five gods are protecting me from the devil. The devil looked back, noticing the other three gods. Oh! The horror, hopefully I can escape his hand. The gods must have something up their sleeves. One of the gods' arrows flew past the devil. In response Satan swung his sickle. They all jumped out of the way and one struck Satan with his sword. “Run!,” I shouted at them, “run! There's no hope, he’s too powerful!”

But they didn’t listen, of course they didn’t listen. Why would gods listen to a mere mortal like me? Satan kicked them away! And started running towards us. One of the gods next to me swung his blade, but it broke against the devil's skin. The other god pulled me back and pointed his weapon at Satan.

Everything around me started getting more and more devilish. The trees smiled at me while bleeding out of all their orises. The snakes started to attack me, ripping my skin out with every bite. The sun was shooting fire at us, everything around burning. I-I just need to get out of here. I can’t just catch fire, I just need to find a way out. But how? I just need to find a way.

I looked over to the hole. That must be my way out! I stepped over the ledge getting ready to jump. But somebody grabbed onto my armor and pulled me back. I’m glad they did because there was a giant mouth in the ground. If I

jumped it would have just swallowed me whole. I would have made it if it wasn't for that. Still peering down I noticed a pool of blood and an army of skeletons. The realm of the gods is really creepy, I can't be here anymore!
"We have to get out of here!" I screamed, "Bring me back to Valor!"

I tried running away but I just fell to the ground. I looked back and watched Satan as kicked a god. He was about to fall but the other caught him. Another of the gods' arrows struck Satan, so he turned around throwing his sickle. Satan started walking towards them as the sickle struck the god. He then proceeded to fall to the ground, dropping his bow.The god grabbed the other god and pulled him up when I looked the other way. The sword and the sickle struck each other over and over again. It all culminated in an explosion. Satan turned around and ran at the god as fast as he could. The god shot at him as he got closer and closer.

Once Satan got to the god he kicked him in the leg. The pain was so intense that he fell to the ground. Satan then kicked him while he was down and turned back to us. I ran to the forest grabbing onto the branch of the crazy tree. It snapped from my weight, I turned around and watched Satan swing his sickle.

The sickle struck the god, bringing it to his knees. The final two gods came running after Satan. He threw his sickle at them, but it got blocked by the sword. The other god shot him in the eye causing Satan to stumble back. But the sickle started coming from behind, thankfully the god blocked it with his sword.

The bottom of the sickle got sliced in half. Sparks flew everywhere, starting a small fire on the ground. The rest of the sickle flew back into Satan's hand. As he was about to throw it again I hit his back with my stick. Satan then stopped, freezing from my strike.

May-maybe I was strong enough to kill him. He's about to fall down dead, stone dead. I can't believe I killed Satan himself. Well, I thought. Satan looked back at me, his beety orange eye glaring. I smacked him again, hitting Satan in his head. The branch snapped from the impact. I then realised I had just made the worst mistake of my life.

"For god's sake," I mumbled to myself.

Blood started running down from my lip. Then, just then was the longest minute of my life. Just Satan staring at me, me staring back. He swung his sickle, I watched in slow-motion as it came down upon me. This is it, this is the end of my life. I tried to save myself, I jumped back. But his sickle still managed to strike me.

With a slight pain in my head everything turned white. A peanut in a tophat wearing a monocle appeared. I can't believe god is just one big peanut. He had this black cane too. He kept swinging it around, looking at me with a strange look. But finally he began to talk.

"Heidy ho Bly," said God, "my name's Cocoa."

Cocoa's a strange name for a god, nevertheless a peanut.

"We're gonna talk while you're laying on the ground over there," said Cocoa.

I responded, "am I dead?"

"Heavens no!" said Cocoa, "You're just a little damaged, you'll be fine. In fact they're rushing you to the hospital right now."

""Well how do you know that?" I asked.

"Think about it," said Cocoa, "I'm just a figment of your

imagination. So you are slightly aware of your surroundings. Even if you're knocked out."

A peanut, Cocoa is making extremely good points right now. Though I guess I'm making those points up myself.

"Are my friends okay?" I asked Cocoa.

Cocoa responded, "I don't' know! I'm you, you're me. So if you don't know I don't know.

"Will I be fine," I asked.

Cocoa responded, "I'm pretty sure, your mentality should be coming back to you."

I'm glad I'll be okay, at least I think. Though Cocoa is a part of my subconscious. Too bad everything's dark, though my vision should be back soon. I've kinda lost feelings in my arms, they hurt a lot, so does my head. Maybe I hit my head on a rock on my way down.

"It looks like I'm gonna have to go," said Cocoa.

I responded, "why?"

"You're waking up," responded Cocoa, "I can't be with you while you're awake."

"I guess I'll see you again sometime," I responded.

"Maybe," said Cocoa, "bye for now."

He disappeared instantly, and I started to open my eyes. The bright white of the hospital shined on my eyes. I grew dizzy sitting up, I looked around the room. It seemed to be the same one Von was in. Though they're all made pretty much the same. Though there was just one difference between now and last time. This time I'm in bed and Von was sitting at my side.

"Look who's awake," said Von.

He seemed to be alright, wearing his brown leather jacket and a white button up shirt. He was also wearing blue

jeans and brown boots. Everything was new besides the jacket. It was stitched where it got scratched up. His eyes were a weird light grey color. The most peculiar thing was that nobody else was there.
"You should be good," said Von.
I responded, "that's good."
"Though," said Von, "there are a few alterations that need to be made to your body."

I looked down at my body and immediately realised why. That must have been why my arms hurt so much. But that got me thinking, at least I'm kinda okay. But what about my friends? What could have possibly happened to them? I know I and Von are gonna be alright but what about them?
"Are they okay?" I asked Von.
He responded with a "well.'
"What!" I said in confusion, "you have to tell me. Are they doing fine? They must be, right?"

Von just kinda sat there doing nothing.

So I asked,

"What happened?"

Part: 6

The gates of no return

Mortem turned around, staring at us. He brought his ax up from the ground, he wanted to kill us. Zach fired another arrow, but it just missed Mortem. Mortem swung his ax at me, but we all jumped out of the way. Ora used the opening to hit Mortem in the shoulder with her sword. Though it only put a small hole into the armor.

“Run!” I heard Bly scream in the background.

Mortem proceeded to kick Zach in the knee. While Zach was down Mortem smacked me and Ora across the face with the bottom of the ax. It struck me first so I took most of the damage. It shattered the left part of my visor and it also destroyed most of that side of the helmet too. It didn’t hit Ora as hard but it was able to knock her helmet off.

Ora helped Zach off the ground as I took off the helmet. Some of the glass got stuck in my skin. Looking ahead Mortem started limping as fast as he could. Syless grabbed onto the back of Bly’s armor and pulled him away from the cliff. Once Mortem got close Raith swung his plasma sword. But the magical armor shattered the plasma blade. Bly started freaking out a lot. He stood up and walked towards the cliff. He looked like he was about to jump but Syless grabbed onto him, causing him to fall back to the ground.

“We have to get out of here!” screamed Bly, “bring me back to Valor!”

I wonder why Bly is acting this way. I hope he’ll be fine, but first we have to stop Mortem. We stood up and started walking towards them. Mortem kicked Raith in the knee, the same way he did to Zach. Raith fell to the ground and Mortem kicked him again. Raith started to fall but Syless managed to grab onto him.

Mortem swung his ax again, missing Syless, and

Zach fired another arrow. It struck Mortem in the elbow, making him distracted as he lit up in flames. Syless managed to pull Raith up and shot Mortem in the eye. Mortem started stepping back distraught. We all realised that Bly had been acting weird, so we looked back and watched him fall while grabbing onto a branch.

Bly fell to the ground, the branch coming down with him. We all heard a buzzing noise, so we looked back at Mortem and watched his ax fly towards us. Me and Ora managed to jump out of the way, but Zach wasn't too lucky. The ax flew into his thigh, cutting it off. Blood was flying everywhere, Zach was screaming from the pain.

I grabbed my medical tape and started wrapping it around his leg. I needed to stop the blood flow so he doesn't die from bleeding out. The ax flew over my head and back into Mortem's hand. Ora got up with her sword in hand while I continued to tend to Zach. Ora's sword struck Mortem's ax and they got into a duel.

Mortem swung at Ora's leg but she blocked it with her sword. Ora proceeded to jump up and strike Mortem in the head. The sword, the ax and the armor all seemed to be made out of the same material. With each strike everything hit got slightly chipped off. Almost as if everything was too powerful. Mortem swung from above, Ora blocking it. She slid her sword out from under the blade of the ax and stabbed Mortem in the side. That gave me an idea to stop Mortem. Just cut the ax heads off the ax with the sword. But in return it could destroy the sword. I looked ahead and watched Syless pick up the plasma sword. He started messing with it before throwing it at Mortem and Ora. But once it got close to Mortem it exploded. Causing Ora to fall

to the ground with burns all across her armor. Mortem turned around and started limping towards Syless. I fired my plasma derringer again, but it just bounced off like usual.
I told Ora, “I have a plan.”
“There is no time for a plan,” said Ora, “right now I just need to keep attacking with the sword, it’s the only thing that can stop him.”

Mortem swung his ax at Syless, but he jumped out of the way. Unfortunately it struck the computer, getting rid of all communication. Mortem swiped at Syless again, but Syless stepped on Mortem’s other side. Mortem turned around and swung his ax overhead. Syless jumped to the side as fast as he could, but he couldn’t fully escape the ax. The ax landed underneath the left shoulder, slicing it off.

From there Syless fell over, landing on his side. Bly ran over to Mortem and hit him with a stick. We all froze as Mortem stood there. I looked down at Syless as he stuck morphine in what’s left of his arm. Bly hit Mortem again, breaking the stick. In response Mortem swung up his ax, cutting off Bly’s lower arms. B;y fell to the ground screaming, hitting his head on a rock.

After that Ora and Mortem went into a full on duel. I ran over to Bly and patched him up, hearing the fight in the background. I then patched up Syless the best I could. And I ran over to them jumping on Mortem’s back. Mortem threw me over his shoulder and I landed on the ground. He swung his ax towards me and Ora stabbed Mortem in the hand.

Mortem dropped the ax, I charged towards it so we could have a chance against this monster. I picked it up and Ora took out the sword. Ora ran towards me, right now it was two to zero. Mortem stuck his hand out and the ax started to shift. The ax flew out of my hand and back into Mortem's. He threw the ax at us, missing both of us. When it was coming back Ora swung her sword. Cutting off most of the ax's staff part, making it a mere hatchet.

Because of that it crashed to the ground, Ora started running towards Mortem. Stabbing Mortem in the gut, and Mortem made a slight hand gesture. Ora knew what this meant so she entered the astral plane and phased through Mortem, watching as the hatchet landed into Mortem's shoulder. The bright orange blood started gushing out of his shoulder and all over his armor. Ora then stepped out of the astral plane, cutting the hatchet off the ax head embedded in Mortem's shoulder.

Unfortunately Mortem caught the ax and the bottom of the ax head stuck into Ora's neck. Ora dropped the sword and grabbed onto her neck. Blood oozed out of both her neck and mouth. With that I realised what was happening. I stood still as Mortem took the ax from her neck. Ora fell to her knees and I embraced her with my arms.

"You know what to do," said Ora, grabbing onto my hand.

She began to turn white as the rest of the blood came pouring out. It was too late to save her, but not too late to stop Mortem.

"Watch over them," said Ora quietly, "commander."

Ora's final words to me was a battlefield promotion. I promise to stop Mortem, for Ora and everyone else who died along the way. I picked up the sword from Ora's side. My body was shaking from fear, it was just me against Mortem. Everything around me started turning black and white, the stars shining upon me. It wasn't just going in and out, It just stayed. My eyes burned from the site of everything. I'm in the Astral Plane.

I turned towards Mortem with the sword in a firm grip. I walked around as he stood there confused. I jumped out of the astral plane, thrusting the sword into Mortem's eye. As he stepped back I slipped back in. Slipping back out I stabbed him in his shoulder. As he swung his ax I slipped back in. I finally had control over it. So I decided to keep using the same strategy.

I got him in his ankle and then his wrist, he dropped his ax in pain. I watched as blood flowed out of everywhere. But I didn't realise that I slipped out and he threw his ax at me so I blocked it with my sword. Unfortunately the momentum of the ax caused the sword to fly out of my hand and it stuck straight in the ground. Mortem proceeded to slam into me, causing me to fall close to the cliff. He swung at me with the sword.

With each swing I got closer and closer to the cliff. But with each swing I also got closer and closer to the hatchet. That's it! That's my way out. He swung at me and I rolled out of the way to the hatchet. I picked it up and swung it into the back of Mortem's leg. He fell due to the pain of it being halfway through.

I pulled it out, taking me to the otherside of the cliff. I swung overhead and he blocked it with the sword. The blade of the sword dug into his hand because it was there to help block. The sword, or the hand, I wonder which one is gonna give out first. So I swung again and again and again and again.

Each strike for something wrong Mortem has done. His hand was heavily gushing blood, I'm surprised he hasn't died by now. I struck again and again, hitting as hard as I could. Each strike chipped away at the hatchet, the sword, and his hand. For Dray, for Seth, for Ora, and everything else he has damaged and destroyed.

I struck again, harder than I ever had before. The sword was almost completely in half. Shards of the sword all over the ground. With one final strike the hatchet went through the sword and into Mortem's shoulder. So I kept striking him again and again. The hatchet getting deeper and deeper into his shoulder. But Mortem managed to stand up, pushing me out of the way.

The hatchet flew out of my hand and fell down the cliff. I looked up at Mortem's mangled body. Blood seeping out of everywhere. His head was leaning over because of the gap between the neck and the shoulder. He just kinda stood there doing nothing, not menacing at all. Mortem picked up the rest of the sword and brought it overhead. Slowly stepping towards me, covered in his own blood. After a few steps he dropped the sword and fell to his knees. Proceeding to fall onto his face, staying there.

"Is this it?" I said quietly to myself.

Did I just kill somebody? No-no don't think of Mortem as a person. He is an evil ruthless god whose only job is to kill. It's a good thing that I killed him. I-I can't believe I killed someone. For the first time I ended someone's life. I can't think like that, by killing him I stopped him from killing tons of other people.

I sat down unable to comprehend what's happening. I heard lots of noises behind me. But I didn't care enough to look. Medical officers ran around me, picking up the people and putting them in stretchers. They seemed to avoid me at first, though I'm in the best condition. After a few minutes two sat down next to me, putting flashlights in my eyes. It stinged a little but wasn't bad.

They checked out my face and my foot. Once they were done they helped me up and put me in one of the transporters. As we flew towards the medical center I noticed they put me with Raith. Probably because he was the second least damaged. Makes sense because they wouldn't have anything to do with him. Besides, he probably only has a broken leg. After a minute we made it to the medical building.

Again they brought me in last, but I'm the least important. I didn't want to but they made me ride in a wheelchair. They said it was because of my foot. Which is a very valid reason. As they wheeled me up to my room I saw the list. Everybody else was four or above. Me and Raith were only two. Though everybody else was missing a limb or two. So they got me into bed and I waited.

After a few hours they put me under anesthesia. They told me they had to remove the glass and stitch me up. Cocoa didn't appear this time, I wonder why. Maybe he's doing something, or maybe the anesthesia isn't as strong. I don't know but an hour later I woke up in the hospital bed. Nobody was at my side this time. But they probably all have to stay in. Or they just can't stand up.

"Just a few hours and I'll be able to see them," I said to myself, "or at least a few of them."

I thought I heard a doctor coming in, but it was just Elaine.

"I thought you were a pharmacist," I said.

"I still am," responded Elaine, "they're just running out of doctors."

I replied, "was it really that bad?"

"Yeah," said Elaine, "looking at your file you seem to be alright. You can go visit Raith right now."

So I got up from my hospital bed. Raith was just a few doors down, so it didn't take too long. Elaine gave me a cane, she said it was for my foot. So I slowly limped over. Walking was a little painful, which made it hard because I couldn't make too many faces. If I did the stitching would pop out. While walking I started thinking about Elaine. I can't think about her, especially since my dead wife is still walking beside me. Besides me, the song is about not letting go. If I don't let go, that song will definitely become my life. All I have to do is let go. I know what I have to do, I just need a few days to figure things out. A few days to find out if my friends are okay. Just a few days, that's all I need. I opened Raith's door and sat down at his bedside.

"Hey man," said Raith, very sickened.

Raith had a cast all up his right leg, probably because Mortem kicked him. Other than that he seemed pretty fine.

"You alright?" I asked.

Raith responded, "Yeah, I only have a broken knee. They said it should be healed by the end of the month."

"That's good," I said, "They said I'm off the hook right now."

"Oh that's great," said Raith.

I think I upset him. Maybe he thought I was bragging. I guess it would make sense, he can't do anything till the end of the month. And I'm all like I can leave today! No wonder he's a little upset, he can't do anything for a little while. Maybe I should stay away from saying things like that to people.

"They said that in a few days I will switch to a brace," said Raith.

"Oh, that's good," I responded, "it seems you're coming

along well.
Raith said, “yeah, but they said I have to keep off my leg. They said my knee was just cracked, so I should be fine in two weeks.”

We wrapped things up after that. I just went on with my days the next two days. Until finally I got to visit Zach and Syless. During those two days I didn’t do much. I just read and planned, though I still don’t know if it will be a good idea. I walked into the building and up to the third floor. I ended up going to Zach first because he was closer. Though Syless was only a few doors down.
“How are you doin’?” I asked.
“I’m doing okay,” said Zach, “they said they’re gonna give me a new leg in a few days.”
“Oh that’s good,” I said.
Zach said, “until then I’m useless. But they said they just have to make one.”
“Gonna need it just right,” I said, “and will probably have a few extra features.”
“Yeah, hidden gun compartment, jet boost. It’s gonna be great,” said Zach.

The leg sounds pretty cool. He probably asked for those features. I wonder what Syless and Bly asked for. I wonder why I can’t see Bly today. Probably because he needs a longer time to heal. That’s okay, I’ll probably be able to see him tomorrow. But after I see him I’m gonna put my plan in fruition. Let’s hope it goes well.
“Man I’m tired,” said Zach, “you seem to be doing fine.”
I responded, “Yeah, just the burn and a little bit of glass.”
“At least you just had to get stitches,” said Zach.
“No,” I said, “I have to apply the burn cream every day.
"“Yeah that seems really difficult,” said Zach.

I responded, “Yeah, you have no idea.”
“Well it was great seeing you,” said Zach.
I responded, “yeah.’
“I guess I’ll,” stuttered Zach, “see you tomorrow.”
“Yeah, well bye,” I said.

So I left the room and walked a few doors down to Syless. The room was the same again. Except it was flipped, mirrored compared to Zach’s. Not to mention Syless is half of Zach’s age. And instead of missing a leg he’s missing an arm. I wonder what kind of attachments he asked for. Probably not a booster, but maybe a bit of storage.
“Look who’s here,” said Syless, “you know this morphine is pretty good.”
“You okay?” I asked.
Syless responded, “I’m fine, just me against the world. Holy shit my arm’s missing! Oh wait-wait I remember.”
So I said, “you seem a little-”
“Out of it!” said Syless.
“Yeah,” I said, “that’s it.”
“You know they’re adding pretty cool things,” said Syless, “there’s gonna be a laser. My arm will just turn into a laser!”
“Sounds great,” I said.
“Not enough morphine,” said Syless, fiddling with the baggie.
I said, “I don’t think you should do that.”
“It’s fine,” said Syless.

The then baggie proceeded to fall to the ground, breaking from the impact. So I grabbed the tissues near the windowsill and cleaned it up. Syless started talking to himself about it. But I decided he’s had enough and didn’t tell the nurse. I didn’t say anything as I left, but he didn’t even notice. After that I went home and started working on my plan. Revising it to make sure it's the best it will ever be. Though I wonder where I'm gonna get all those flowers. Thankfully the next day Bly was ready for visitors, so I went and said hi to him.

This time he was on the third floor instead of the second. When I walked in I realised it was like the same room I was in. It definitely looked like his arms were prepped for the operation. Though he was sleeping, I sat there for a few minutes. He ended up waking up eventually.

I said, "Look who's awake."

He was still waking up and seemed kinda confused. I felt like I should say something but I didn't know what. So I figured I would tell him something I already know. But what? Probably something about him that seems to make the most sense to me.

"You should be good," I said.

Bly responded, "That's good."

"Though," I said, "there are a few alterations that need to be made to your body."

Bly looked down at his arms and immediately realised what was wrong. His arms were missing, well his forearms. He didn't seem very surprised, he probably didn't know what was wrong with his arms. But he at least knew something. I wonder why they didn't wait to ask him why. They probably ran out of time and had to get it done right away. So they probably don't have any special features.

"Are they okay?" Asked Bly.

I responded with "well."

"What!" he said in confusion, "you have to tell me. Are they doing fine? They must be, right?"

I just kinda stood there silent not knowing what to say.

Yes they're alive, but they're not really fine. Besides, he doesn't even know about Ora. So I don't really even know what to say. How will I tell him I'm the new commander? He definitely started to get worried.
"What happened?" he asked.

So I started to tell him what happened. All in my perspective, so I turned on my tape recorder and started to have fun. Though I just told him about the fight.

Now to get to my plan, I just need a lot of flowers. I need two thousand six hundred and ninety-four flowers. All spread out between nine bouquets. I went to the flower shop and got them in the colors of pink, purple, and white. I walked up to the waterfall and set up eight of the bouquets. Four on each side of a tree. The fish were a lot calmer today, though it's not raining and the stream's steady.

I got some guy named Zeck to give Elaine a map. A map that should lead to here. So I sat there waiting for about half an hour. At the end of that Zeck used his walky talky to tell me she's coming. So I left and made my way to the hot air balloon. By the time I flew towards her she should be here. But I only have ten minutes so I need to move fast.

I got to the "hot air balloon", I only say that because it's not really a hot air balloon. It just keeps the same name to avoid confusion. It just works like a regular ship. The plasma compulsion isn't as strong so it doesn't go as fast. Don't want to fly out of the little basket-like structure. They just add a cloth balloon to make it appear as a hot air balloon.

On fancier planets they just use the basket like structures. But it's mainly for leaders to make speeches. On president Seaburg's planet Nassor there is a whole chamber of them. In the middle is one big one for Seaburg and his guards. It's mainly bigger to show power and it has a built in force field to protect him.

Anyways I started ascending, eventually steady enough to go straight. Once I got close enough to the waterfall I started descending. With my bouquet in hand I noticed Elaine below. So I carefully landed close to the flowers. I opened the gate and handed the bouquet to Elaine. She was completely and utterly shocked. I was standing there when I was like oh yeah I should say something. Man, I haven't done this in a while.

"Wanna go on a date?" I asked.

"Um," she stuttered, "sure."

I responded, "neat."

The next few days me and Elaine were extremely happy. Eating dinner, seeing sites. But eventually the others were healed up. So we had to go to Ora's and Dray's funeral. I didn't have any suits, so I went to the tailor shop. I got a dark black suit with a dark grey dress shirt. A black tie, boots and belt to finish it off. The finishing touch was a gold pin signifying me as commander.

Syless had an all black suit with a crimson tie. It's just like what he would usually wear, just more dressy. The only things of note was his silver left hand and a pin, signifying he's a medic. He's been going to school to make up for Dray dying. Bly was wearing a white suit with a black dress shirt and tie. Again the metal hands stood out along with the pin signifying he was a captain.

Raith was wearing a dark grey suit with a white shirt and black tie. He didn't have any metal limbs, but he didn't lose one. His pin showed that he was a sergeant. Zach was wearing a black suit and white dress shirt. He also had a black bow tie and a cane topped with a gold crest. His pin showed that he was a major.

We all rode in the same carrier. It was like the hot air balloon except it's only a foot off the ground. It was more of a square shape with walls and windows. It also has a roof, though that's self explanatory. The seats were comfortable and a nice dark blue. Though for some reason Elaine wasn't allowed to be in with us.

"Been here for over a week and you already have a girl," mocked Syless.

Bly responded, "especially since it's against the code."

"Even though you're a commander," said Raith, "you still have to abide by the rules."

"I didn't know that was a rule," I said.

Bly responded, "did you not go over the rules?"

"I didn't have time," I said, "I just haven't been able to go through it yet, I've been really busy."

"That's not a good excuse," asserted Bly.

"You're completely disobeying rules made by president Seaburg," said Raith.

I sat there quite not knowing what to say. They're just attacking me for something I had no idea about. It was mainly just Raith complaining about how we need to stay faithful to the U.G.C. I'm surprised because I figured Bly would be more adamant in the conversation. He likes the U.G.C the most between all of us.

"You know I figured Syless would do something like this, not you," said Raith, "I won't be surprised if you're actually a rebel."

Bly spoke out, "oh just leave him alone!"

"Why he's not fit to be a commander!" screamed Raith, "that position should have gone to you."
"I didn't want this," I told Raith, "Ora chose me to lead you guys. She thought I was good enough to do this. So if you stand in my way, I will rain hell down upon you!" Cringe.
Raith responded, "who cares, we're here anyways."

The ceremony was great besides Raith ignoring me. He believes in more of a strong leader to control. But I really don't need to be that controlling. The minister was really devoted to his speech for Ora and Dray. We got to say our final goodbyes while looking into the pods. Though it was weird doing it at Dray's, since you know, he doesn't have a head. But by the end of it the pods got sent out to space. With fireworks in the night sky.

After the ceremony when everyone was gone we started walking back to the ship. But we got ambushed by U.G.C soldiers. They surrounded us with their guns pointed at us. Shocked, I stood still doing nothing. Why would they just try to capture us? We're on the same team. Is it something we've done? I can't think of anything that we could have possibly done wrong. But they clearly don't care, did one of them do something?
"You're under arrest," said one of the guards, "for committing war crimes and the destruction of nature."
"Commander?" asked Syless.
The guard responded, "stay silent, everything you say or do can be used against you in the court of the Iskels."

All of a sudden a big flare appeared out of nowhere. It burned my eyes with fury. So much so I fell to the ground, the flame breaching to my skin. I felt pain on my whole left side. Once it disappeared Syless was gone. The rest of us were standing there with burned suits and armor. The metal limbs glew orange from the heat, as well as the soldiers' guns.

"Okay, Okay, you're coming with us," said the soldiers.

By the morning we all sat in a cell, the same burnt clothes from the night before. Syless is still missing, until they find him we're stuck. While awaiting the trial they gave us food and water. Though of course it's terrible, but it's all we have. After a while they just decided to do the trial and let Syless go. They brought us into the Iskels chamber. The four of us brought to our knees. The three Iskels stared down at us with rage. Except one who just sat there doing nothing. It was also extremely dark, apparently light from the suns would kill them.

"Don't say that green!" said the red one, "we need to give them a chance."

"A chance!" said the blue one, "they destroyed our sacred land!"

Red responded, "what if they had a reason. Yes green I know they awakened Mortem."

"We didn't awaken Mortem!" yelled Bly.

"Just shut up!" yelled blue, "I say we just kill them!"

"That's crazy green!" yelled red while gripping onto green's neck.

Blue responded, "it's perfectly fine to suggest that."

"I can't believe they're in charge," I said.

"Besides," said Red, "what if the N.G.C's resurrected Mortem."

Blue and green started to calm down, maybe red brought up a good point. But out of nowhere Red gripped onto Green's neck and wouldn't let go. Green's eyes started going white as we heard stuff behind us. Blue tried fending off Red but Red kicked him away. Then the door behind us bursted open, plasma beams flying across the room. One of them hit Green's shoulder, causing him to slump down.

Another beam hit the window, shattering it. The light instantly flooded in, Red turning around and putting his hands up. His screams were muted by him turning into stone. Blue tried to escape falling off his chair, Zach used his metal leg and caved in Blue's head. The blood began to ooze all over the ground. A light noise mumbled from Green's throat, but it was all he could muster. Slowly turning to stone as the light flooded through his chair.

The scene was horrific as the roof started collapsing. Dust sifted down as I looked up. One of the wooden beams got shot and started falling down. Eventually crashing down, causing Green and Blue to fully turn into stone. The rest of the roof caved in because there was no support. Crashing down onto us, knocking us out.

Eventually I woke up later that day, the whole roof had fallen down. My brand new shirt was destroyed by now. All holey and tattered, I was even missing my pin. I stood up and watched as these soldiers attacked. Fighting any military authority there was. All citizens seemed safe from harm and they appeared to be coming down from a mother ship. I could see it very clearly in the distance. It had a huge base with a giant tower. It was almost a citadel attached to the side of a volcano. It was wacky and the ships came from inside the volcano. One of the soldiers walked up to me and made sure I was okay. They seemed to be very nice, it was almost as if they were liberating us from the U.G.C's rule. I wonder how they're gonna respond.

The others started waking up around me. More and

more guards walked up and checked on us. Once we were all up and good the guards escorted us down. Getting all of us out of the building and to the outside. By the end of the day the mother ship started coming down. Eventually crashing down upon the government building.

The guards escorted us to get our stuff. So I removed my suit jacket and put on my leather one. Eventually grabbing all my stuff as the guard escorted me and Elaine to our room. The tower was ginormous, going up past the clouds. It was a bright and shiny silver, with crimson glass on each round corner. There's eight balconies on each floor, one for each room. With one hundred floors there's five-hundred and twenty rooms, all contained within sixty-five floors. The other thirty-five floors contain schools, training faculties, laundry rooms, restaurants, etc.

During the next few days they broke down the buildings and developed a nice space. I read a lot during that time, mainly the books I picked up from the library nearly a week ago. Me and the others got enlisted into this new military. They said our main goal was to finish off the rest of the N.G.C. Apparently members of our old military weren't killed. They were just knocked out and re-witted.

Mine and Elaine's relationship grew a lot during this time. Though everytime we go out that song seeps into my mind. Like this one time we were having dinner, overlooking the top of the volcano. It was a beauty, I tried using it to distract myself but it didn't work.

When the wind blows

Deep at night

Sitting by the fire

Warmness on my feet
Before the wind dies down
But at least I still
Have you besides me

Oh why can't I get you out of my head!

When the wind blows
Deep at night
The days almost near
The winds gone down
But you're still beside me

I'm just trying to have a good time. But it's like I'm still not over it, why?

When the wind blows
Deep at night
The days almost near
The winds gone down
But you're still beside me

I-I just can't do this, I don't think I'm ready. But how can I possibly know if I am. I excused myself from the dinner and went to the bathroom. Turning on the faucet and splashing water on my face. I got some on my black t-shirt though my jacket caught most of it. But it just wouldn't slip out of my mind. The more water I splashed on, the more muted it got. But it still didn't go away. I just need it to go away, but it just won't. It just stays and I can't get rid of it.

The air is steady
In the mid-day
A drop of rain comes down
Sending chills down my spine
The sad thing is that
You're not besides me

I wiped the water off my face and I walked back to the table. Looking down at the volcano, bubbling at its non-active surface. Finishing our dinner while having a small conversation. Over the next week we had a few more dates but the song was still stuck, just the beginning though. But on the final day, three weeks since I first got on Valor. It stopped, I think I'm finally at peace.

That day was really worrying, mainly because Syless had been missing for nearly two weeks. He just disappeared, nowhere in sight. I just can't imagine where exactly he went. During the rest of the day they took us on a tour of the volcano. It was all one big hangar with a big door. Several smaller doors above that too. There were three floors and the guide was going to take us through them all.

First was the biggest one that held all the big ships. He showed us the tri-winged transporter shuttle ship. It had three wings, two on each of the sides and one on top. It was dark grey with dark blue stripes across the wings and sides. It had four plasma compulsers with two on each side. The wind shield was split in two. I don't know why it's called a windshield, there's no wind in space. Though I guess it's also used to transport inside of planets too.
"This ship is mainly used to transport people from place to place," said the guide, "though it's also really used to

smuggle people from place to place where they're not supposed to be."

There was a whole line of them going down. Once they got to the center the ships changed direction to the otherside. Probably because there's a door on the other side as well. There were two more ships on this level they wanted to show us. So we decided to go to them straight away.

"Next is the king's ship," said the guide, " he uses it to cruise across the galaxy when he doesn't want to be stuck in the tower."

It was huge, nearly as long as the base. It was greyish with red stripes. Peaking through the windows you could see all the luxury rooms and dinners. Almost the whole inside was a crimson with lush dark blue padding. All lined with a gold crest, revealing the king's insignia. It had four large plasma compulsers. It also has three wings, one on top and two on each side. But they're towards the back and not very big compared to the rest of it. This ship is the reason why the door is so big, it must be amazing to stay in one of those.

The guide said, "quite an exquisite ship in'it. Next are the two frater cargo ships. Used to transport all the goods from planet to planet. All the ones we liberated from the U.G.C's grasp. Making this planet the capitol will be quite challenging, but we will manage."

The frater cargo ships were half the size of the king's cruiser. They only had a somewhat large cabin space. But the rest of it was a bunch of cargo space. It's very thin and has lots of cables to keep it in place.

"Next we'll be going up a level," said the guide.

So we walked up bright yellow stairs right next to the door. It's a really thick door to protect against bombs. It can also be locked by a computer room somewhere in the tower. We walked up the stairs to grated bridge pathways. There's a bunch of fighters hanging off the ceiling. The pathways going in between each of them. With little stairs going up to each cockpit. With five ship classes it was truly a wonder to behold.

"First is the A1-750," said the guide, "It's used for fast pace infiltration of enemy bases."

They were super small, only meant for one person. They are so small there are at least one hundred right there. The base was triangular with the same three fins, just like all the other ships. This one has a green stripe and a medium sized plasma compulser on the side fins. The top one had two really small ones on each side of it.

The guide said, "It's truly an excellent ship."

"I can't wait to use one of those," said Bly.

"The next one is the smallest of the five," said the guide, "but by far the fastest. The A2-570 is good to get in and out as fast as possible. It's the one most used by us, perfect for our strategies."

There's twice as many as the other kind of ship. It was basically the same thing as the other one. Except that it's a lot smaller and has a lot more smaller plasma compulsers. Two on each side wing and four on the top one. Topped off with a vibrant orange stripe, definitely the least interesting of the five ships.

"Then there's the A3-630," said the guide, "definitely the heaviest, gun wise of all the ships. The power is really useful for conq-liberating other planets."

This ship was big and bulky, you could tell it had a lot

of power. It was white with grey spots on it. This one only had the two side fins and seated two people. It had two giant plasma compulsers on each fin, with two smaller ones next to it. It had a nice burgundy stripe, upon closer inspection it had a really small top fin. Though it's a lot smaller than the guns. The other two only had one on each side wing. It had two on each side wing, one on each side of the really small fin. And then two at the nose of the ship. They were only able to fit fifty onto this line, but they're so big they just take up that much space. So far their aviation armory is extremely strong.

"The A4-920 has only one purpose," said the guide, "to go up and blow up stuff. It's the second smallest only because of its bomb. Though only robots pilot these ships so you don't have to worry."

Tik-tok tik-tok tik-tok

Oh-uh these ships are like a tiny A3, except it doesn't have all the guns and has much smaller boosters. With no cockpit the nose of the ship is much smaller than all the other ones. Though it's still arrow dynamic, there's also a tiny camera to allow the robot to see. There were almost as many of these as there were A2's. Accompanied by a nice yellow stripe, suits well for the explosions.

"Finally the final one on this floor, the A5-860," said the guide, "it's the least used of all our ships. But it's also the least useful, especially if you want to liberate the planet. It both shoots out fire to burn everything in its path and drops water to put it out."

Tik-tok tik-tok tik-tok

It-uh is definitely the ship Syless would like the most. Too bad he's not here to see it, hiding somewhere. Also it's kinda dumb to have a bunch of gasoline next to something that explodes, with a bunch of lava above it as well. On one side it had a black stripe and on the other white. There were a little less of them than the A1's, but they were just slightly bigger too.

"Now let's go up these stairs to the final floor," said the guide.

Tick-tock tick, tock

We-we walk up the bright yellow stairs to the final floor. It was just one big room with a bunch of little tiny ships grouped within fences. But looking up was a round transparent roof, except the edges. But just above the blue roof was lava. Apparently the clear blue roof is a forcefield, used to protect everything from the lava. But it's kinda dumb because if someone shuts down the forcefield all the ships inside will be destroyed. Not a good idea, I can't wait to get out of here.

"As you can see," said the guide, "most of these ships appear to be very similar. For the most part, yes. They all have red and blue stripes, red to show the king's power and blue for solomon occasions."

They really do appear to be the same. But they must be separated for a reason. Otherwise it's just a waste of materials. Especially with lava right above it. Sorry, I'm still kind of stumped on that. I don't know, at least I'm able to focus on something today. For some reason I've had trouble with that today.

Tik-tok tik, tok tik, tok

"Between the eight types this is the first one. The E3-2020 mostly used by King Rex himself," said the guide, "It's perfect for giving speeches from high up, and even has a place for itself in President Seaburg's chamber. With built in force fields to protect him from being harmed."

It was kinda like the one I used, except for it's crest and stripe. Now that I look at all the ships there is something different about each of them. They all have different crests at the front, probably to show what kind of authority is using it. It would make the most sense to me.

"Next is the E4-1220, with a different crest to signify that higher up guards are using it," said the guide.

I was right! *Tik-tok* I knew that had something to do with the crests, but what else would it signify? It just wouldn't be fancy things to put on for no reason. *Tik, tok* I don't know, maybe I'm just very good at guessing how things are.

The guide said, "Next is my ship, the E5-220, as you can tell by its insignia. But it's mainly used for me to use for speeches while our king can't. With a few extras just in case the one in front stops working. It can also be used to shut down anything in the base to kill our enemies while we make our escape."

"Must not have needed to use it, huh?" asked Bly.

The guide responded, "of course, this base is still here."

"Then there's the E7-850," said the guide, "it's used by our police force which is why it shows their insignia. They use it to control the public during speeches so they don't try to attack the king. Also used during riots to control the public."

Tik, tok Tik, tok Tik, tok

"The E8-420 is the next ship. Mainly used for public transport," said the guide,

A soldier asked, "So we can take one any time we want to explore the planet?"

"Yes," said the guide, "But you'll need to have a pass, which you can only get if you're considered a trustworthy citizen."

"These are one special kind of these ships," said the guide, "Used by robots the E9-405 is a surveillance drone.

Monitoring the outside of the volcano and tower to make sure there will be no attacks."

Tik-tok tik-tok tik, tok

"This one is definitely the most sneaky of the eight," the guide stated, "The E10-180 has a built in visible distorter making it almost impossible to see by the naked eye. Used for spying on our enemies."

The last two definitely have more of a military aspect to them. But with the state of King Rex's Potentate it makes sense they have these in case the U.G.C attacks. Especially since they liberate U.G.C planets. So I guess they have that going for them. Though they aren't mentioned that much because the U.G.C doesn't consider them a threat. They just let them liberate their planets.

Tik, tok tik, tok tik, tok

"Finally," said the guide, "The E12-550 is the most different of all of them. They have a special force field that allows the people inside to go into space. It also has little arms so we can fix ships while they are still in space. They're really useful but only used by engineers."

It probably is the most different compared to all the other ones. But I don't know why they'd do that one last. I guess that's the way we went. After that the guide walked us out of the volcano. My watch they gave me beeped to tell me to go to lunch. So I took the elevator up to Royalty Dinner, where I sat down across from Raith.

Tik, tok tik, tok

"Did you hear?' asked Raith.

I responded, "what?"

"Zach was hospitalized," said Raith, "for trying to commit suicide."

"What!" I said.

The clock kept ticking and tocking. They have been really loud all day, this one especially. It's completely annoying and brings my mind into dark places. Which is a terrible thing to happen when you're trying to talk to your friend. Talking about something that is extremely upsetting. Why can't the tick-tocks go away?

Tik, tok Tik, tok

"Apparently the whole Mortem thing really messed him up," said Raith. "He got all depressed and couldn't think straight. All the sounds around him were amplified, it drove him crazy."

I responded, "That sounds really bad."

Tik, tok tik, tok tik, tok

"Yeah, he kept saying something about a clock," said Raith.

Tik, tok tik, tok

"Oh-man," said Raith, "You look a little woozy, I think you had too many drinks."

"No-no I'm fine," I slurred.

Tik, tok tik, tok tik, tok tik, tok

Raith said, " Okay go back to your room."

"Fine," I said. "Fine."

"Don't worry I'll pay," smirked Raith.

I stumbled my way to my room, walking to my wood grain table. The clock is getting louder and louder. There's not even a clock in the room and it's still there. I finally escaped the grasp of the song and the clock challenged it. The image of Mortem stays in my mind and I can't get rid of it. The dented helmet and the body splitting at the shoulder. The blood oozing out of every gap in his armor. Nerves and bones sticking out of the gash, nearly two feet big. The large bull horn and his destroyed lower left leg. All the holes in his chest and stomach from where I stabbed him. Bits of the ax and the sword stuck in him from chipping off. The battle worn ax stained with blood. I threw up from the thought of it. I looked up into the mirror, looking into my white eyes. I haven't been able to use the astral plane since that day and I don't think I want to. Gazing closer into the mirror I noticed something. Two people were standing there, or at least one and a half anyways. I turned around to reveal the dead corpses of Ora and Dray standing there. I threw up again, how are they even there?

"Hello there," said Ora.

What! They-they can talk, my own mind is talking to me. How is this even possible? My own mind is creating figments of my imagination. Spooking me, maybe I am turning insane. I'm going to end up just like Zach, no-no it can't be.

"Let us go," gasped Dray.

Ora then stated, "re-enter the astral plane."

"No," I said, "I can't."

"You have too," gasped Ora.

"Get out of my head!" I screamed, "get out of my head!"

Dray moaned, "he's not going to do it."

"We just have to wait," gasped Ora, "We just have to wait."

"Let's hope it's not for long," said Dray.

They disappeared. Either I'm going crazy or I'm extremely drunk. Though it doesn't matter, that clock just keeps ticking. So I took out my bottle of whiskey and started to drink it. Sitting at my desk and looking at my face. The smooth alcohol slipped down my throat, adding a sense of relief with each sip.

But after a while I started thinking about my life. My relationship with Elaine has fallen apart. She started sleeping in one of her friends' second room. She said she was uncomfortable with all my drinking. But I wasn't being very kind to her anyways. I looked back into the mirror and Mortem was staring at me through it. I got so scared I fell back onto the ground, breaking the chair.

Tik-tok tik, tok

The clock raged with noise at me, Mortem still staring. So I threw my whiskey bottle at it, smashing against the wall. The mirror was cracked, but Mortem was still there. So I picked up the mirror with my right hand and smashed it against the table. I flipped it over with Mortem still there, his crimson eyes glowing. So I smashed it against the table again and again.

Tik, tok tik-tok tik-tok

The second time it bounced out of my hand and leaned against the wall. But Mortem was still within the shattered glass. So I smashed it against my knee, breaking it in half. Injured, I sat down on my chair turned stool at my cracked desk. Looking at my yellow stained wall, playing with the broken bottle with my blood stained hand. My knee hurts from the piece of glass stuck into it. The jeans all ripped and cut up from the glass. So I started playing with the dagger that Bly gave me a few days ago. He wanted me to study it, or something along those lines.

Tik-tok tik, tok tik-tok tik, tok

"You just need to hold out a little longer," said Ora from behind me, "you need to save us Von, you need to save us."

I took my leather jacket off and threw it at Ora. Going straight through her and hitting the painting behind her. The painting crashed down to the ground, breaking. Ora didn't even flinch, it was almost as if she was a ghost. No she's not a ghost, she's just a figment of my imagination. She's not even there, I just need to ignore her.

"We can't break free when you're like this," said Ora.

I responded, "Get out of my head!"

I sat back down on the desk, almost breaking the chair. My mind began to wander, why am I here? I can't do this anymore, I need to be back with my wife. I picked up the dagger that Bly gave me. Putting it to my left wrist, slowly sliding it down. The blood slowly trickled out, eventually spraying all over the desk. Continuing to spray as the dagger left my wrist. With all the blood coming out I became light headed. I stabbed the desk, causing it to shift. My vision started getting extremely blurry. Blood seeping through the cracks of the desk. The sound of it hitting the ground aggravating me, but I did nothing. I couldn't do anything, I was getting too weak. My hand loosened from the dagger as I placed my elbow on the table. The dagger dislodged itself causing me to fall. Crashing into the table, it broke from my weight. I fell to the ground very nearly blacking out. As my eyes started closing, someone came into the room.

"Are you okay?" asked someone, "we heard a lot of noise over here."

"Von!" someone else screamed.

Eventually I blacked out, waking in a bed in a hospital room. Zach in one right across from the room. Bly and Raith sat at my bedside. There were tubes in my arms and I was wearing red medical clothes. Bly was wearing a white button up shirt and black jeans. Raith was wearing a black button up shirt and black jeans. They seemed a little worried, but

I'm doing all right. Though I'm wondering how long I'm going to be here, probably until they find me fit to leave. Hopefully not for too long, maybe just a few days.
"How are you doing?" asked Bly.
I responded, "I think I'm doing just fine."
"That's good," said Raith, "Your life is starting to sound like that song you sing all the time."

The airs just fine
In the evening
But the pain's not leaving
So I joined the army
But that wasn't very long
'Cause I got gunned down
But now, I'll finally be free
'Cause I'll finally be with you again.

Oh god, he's right. My life is exactly like that song, well not exactly. I tried killing myself, I wasn't shot down by N.G.C's. So maybe he isn't right, and that's a good thing. That song was out of my mind for so long until he said something, but it didn't stay for long. Only because I need to remember that I need to move on. If I don't I won't be going anywhere, changing is the only thing that's going to lead me away.
"They said you should be out in a few weeks," said Raith.
"Oh," I said, "okay, that sounds good."
Bly said, "let's go sit on the balcony."

So I got up off my bed and dragged the tube stand with me. The doors sliding open, a force field was around the balcony. But that makes sense to me, I slid down the tube stand till I got to the ground. The others went down very easily, but their knees weren't injured. We watched the sun set under the horizon. The day is ending and week four is beginning, I prepared to say something by putting my hand on Raith's shoulder.

"So what was the lie?" I asked.

"Wess," said Raith, "He's alive."

Epilogue

Captain's log number three, star date 2694. Thirty days in. During these last three weeks I learned a lot of things. I pushed back a lot of these things for nearly three weeks but yesterday brought them back out again. Von just laying there, nearly dead. It made me realise again, that life and death aren't two parts of the equation. They're the same thing, just a few acute differences.

They both have something to do with living beings. Making their one-way trip through our known universe. What's before and after are both unknown. The past few weeks have been hard without Ora and Dray. But I've managed to hold back my feelings around other people, but when I'm alone I think about them.

It's hard, extremely hard, and Von has lost more in three weeks than I have since I joined army school. Unfortunately he couldn't take it, and most people can't. He was just lucky enough to be found in time. As much as you want to leave something behind, you shouldn't. You shouldn't completely forget, you should look back and be happy that you were together for when you were. But you also shouldn't let it dominate your entire life.

I'm nervous for what's to come, who knows what's next. Whatever it is, something doesn't feel right. Maybe it's the losses, maybe because everythings changing. Von's going to have a tough time being the new commander. I don't think he's fit, but Ora chose him. And I need to respect Ora's dying wish. Besides, maybe he will be great at it. But between the last remaining N.G.C's and the looming threat of the tyrannical fascism of King Rex's Potentate. It will be a difficult job for Von to take on, but I think that he'll make it.

Von still believes in the good of a lot of things in the universe. He thinks the U.G.C isn't a fasciast dictatorship just like King Rex's Potentate. He doesn't even know the Potentate is a faciast dictatorship. But when time comes he will realise that not everything is as they seem. And I'm afraid that things aren't what they seem. My gut was right with Seth and I think it's right with this. Big changes are about to come, but the question is that if we're doing the right thing.

www.ingramcontent.com/pod-product-compliance
Lightning Source LLC
LaVergne TN
LVHW010548160826
845677LV00013B/3040

* 9 7 9 8 8 4 4 0 8 0 3 9 5 *